# WULFGAR AND THE RIDDLE

# WULFGAR AND THE RIDDLE

Christina Eastwood

Christian Year Publications

ISBN-13: 978 1 914273 07 0

Copyright © 2021 by Christian Year Publications
40 Beansburn, Kilmarnock, Scotland

All rights reserved. No part of this publication may be reproduced, stored in a retrieval system, or transmitted in any form or by any other means – electronic, mechanical, photocopy, recording or otherwise – without prior permission of the copyright owner.

Typeset by John Ritchie Ltd., Kilmarnock
Printed by Bell & Bain Ltd., Glasgow

# Contents

Foreword 7

Dedication 8

Acknowledgements 9

Introduction 11

**Chapter One**
The Road 13

**Chapter Two**
Homecoming 21

**Chapter Three**
Leofham Burgh 33

**Chapter Four**
Old Friends and a New Job 45

**Chapter Five**
The Riddling Nun 55

**Chapter Six**
Shaftesbury 63

**Chapter Seven**
Æthelgifu and Eadwulfu 67

**Chapter Eight**
Embroidery 73

**Chapter Nine**
Leofrun 81

**Chapter Ten**
The Scriptorium 85

**Chapter Eleven**
The Go-Between 91

**Chapter Twelve**
The Dragon Speaks 97

**Chapter Thirteen**
A Plan 101

**Chapter Fourteen**
Escape 107

**Chapter Fifteen**
Caught! 115

**Chapter Sixteen**
The King 121

**Chapter Seventeen**
Adam 129

Glossary 139

# Foreword

In this adventure, Wulfgar, the hero invented by Christina Eastwood for these stories, returns to Wessex, which I love as my own native area, and quickly becomes aware of differences of thought and outlook from his sojourn in East Francia, in the area we now call France. He meets other people, including some who actually lived in history, such as King Alfred the Great, Æthelgifu the King's daughter, and Asser the Welsh monk who was Bishop of Sherborne, knew Alfred, and wrote the earliest story of Alfred's life. In the course of Wulfgar's travels, adventures and work, he muses on different ways of thought and worship he has encountered in both Francia and Wessex, and wrestles with the question of how he himself should think, especially as to what he can trust to lead him and others towards true belief. His questions are ones people still ask and debate today, and it is as important now as it has ever been for us to search for answers to them.

David M. Young, MA, MPhil,

former Director of the Albanian Evangelical Mission and author of *Mission to Albania, The Great River, Change and Decay* and *Primitive Methodism from Late Victorian Times Till World War One*

## DEDICATION

To

Eleanor Faith Jones

Welcome, welcome, little one,
Welcome to the sky, the trees, the birds, the sun,
Welcome to the grief, the pain, the woe, the loss,
But welcome to the road to heaven through Christ's cross.

With love
From
Nain

## ACKNOWLEDGEMENTS

Thanks are due to Gerallt Jones, Pant Glas, for checking and correcting the Welsh phrases in this book, to Philip Bell for suggestions and to David Young for historical advice.

# Introduction

If you have read the two previous books *Wulfgar and the Vikings* and *Wulfgar and the Dragon*, you will remember that Wulfgar was "banished" to East Francia to learn his craft by the king, who could have inflicted a much worse punishment on him. You will also remember his friend Morcant the Celt who escaped from the Vikings in the first book in the series.

Wulfgar is back from his travels in Francia and he has learned a lot while he has been away. But perhaps some of the ideas he has accepted are not as good as those he left behind in Wessex.

Just as he is beginning to find the answers to the riddle that confronts him he's caught up in an escapade that is definitely against the law – or is it?

On the front of this book you can see a picture of an Anglo-Saxon aestel or reader's pointer. Some people think the picture on it is of King Alfred himself. Certainly it is one of several that the king gave with his Latin translations to every bishopric in his kingdom. Perhaps it is the one that peeps into the story!

# Chapter 1
# The Road

This is the record of Wulfgar Waelwulfson of Leofham Burgh in Wessex, master wood carver, detailing the mercy of God to his creatures in the Kingdom of Wessex and elsewhere. The said Wulfgar, having served eight years under Abbot Bovo of Corvey in East Francia to learn his craft, was summoned thence by his Lord, Alfred, King of the Anglo-Saxons.

Two of us had travelled together from Corvey in East Francia, myself, on my way to my home village of Leofham, and a young Frankish monk called Grifo who was going to the Abbey at Æt Baðum. Poor man, he had been horribly seasick when we crossed the South Sea from the coast of Francia and he was little better once we were on dry land again. I wondered what to do. He was not well enough to travel on foot but I was impatient to be setting out on the last stage of my journey. I had grown very fond of brother Grifo as we crossed Francia together but he, lying green faced and miserable on a pallet bed in the cottage of a widow who lived near the place where we had landed, urged me to go on with my journey at once. The widow would take care of him for a little money, he said, and in any case our paths would surely have diverged quite soon.

I agonised. Did the polite and cultured Brother Grifo know what he was letting himself in for by coming to Wessex? How would he fare on his own? He certainly did not know about sea voyages. He was astonished to find the boat had made him so sick. Not for the first time in our travels together I wondered if he should have stayed where he was more at home. I had tried to explain to him that Wessex was not like Francia as we travelled on foot together from Corvey but I found it hard to put the differences into words that did not make my own dear Wessex sound – well – a little bit rough and unpolished. Now we were actually in Wessex I worried about leaving him alone. "Shall I wait with you?" I asked again. "It will be no trouble and you'll feel better in a matter of hours."

"No, no," he groaned quietly, "I'll be fine but I've never felt so terrible. I'm sure it will take some time for this to get better – tomorrow or next week and then I'll set off."

The widow woman offered to find someone to guide him when he was feeling better and, in the end, I set off alone.

It was April, the beginning of the year, a joyful time to be coming back to Leofham. The song of the throstles and blackbirds in the hedges and copses was a cheerful welcome. Eight years was a long time. I strode along the downland trackway and into the overhanging shadows of the forest, my bag of tools over my shoulder and a little gold left from my wages tucked into my tunic and I must admit that Brother Gifo slipped from my mind at first. As I marched along the long road towards home, I gave myself up to pleasant considerations: I would give the simple peasants with whom I grew up quite a surprise when I got there – I was a master craftsman now!

But I soon began to miss my walking companion, and to enjoy being alone with my own thoughts less. I thought over some of the things the two of us had chatted about to pass the time while we were still walking through Francia. At first we had been with a group of monks returning to Corbie Abbey in East Francia but our paths had diverged after a few days and Brother Grifo and I were left to make our own way to the coast. One day I had entertained him with the story of my adventures, some years ago, with a dragon that had suddenly appeared near our village – well, two dragons actually – and he was very interested. Dragons were apparently not uncommon in remote parts of Francia, but he had never seen one himself. He was an earnest and scholarly young man and he eagerly pumped me for every detail of the dragons' appearance.

"I have only seen them in pictures myself," he had explained, "and I am keen to know just how true to life our artists have made them."

I had tried hard to give him some impression of size. "We set up the leg bones over the thane's chair in the village Mead Hall in the end," I explained, "and King Alfred himself even sat under them when he was there!"

"Ah yes, The king! You told me, I think, that you were sent to Francia by royal command to work on the building of our Abbey at Corvey. I don't think I took in what you were saying. Do you mean it was actually King Alfred himself who sent you?" Brother Grifo had asked as we strode along in the spring sunshine, past prosperous fields and newly cleared woodland. "However did that come about?"

The circumstances of my despatch to Francia were not a little embarrassing and I had not wanted Brother Grifo to question me in more detail! "Yes, he did," I replied, then quickly changing the subject, I added, "and I arrived when the building was nearing completion so I was able to work alongside masters of their craft in furnishing the inside. I had never seen such a magnificent construction or such a rich interior in my life before. The Westwerk alone is an imposing structure without mentioning the rest of the building!"

Brother Grifo had smiled, quietly proud of his countrymen and an awkward moment had been avoided.

These reflections banished my loneliness a little. If Brother Grifo had been with me now I would have pointed out the good quality of the new road to him, I thought, as I entered the forest.

The dappled shade of the trees was agreeable and soon other cheerful ideas occurred to me. I patted my big pocket contentedly as I thought of what it contained. Alongside my tools I had a gift for my friend Morcant that I knew would interest him: a small book. I was sure ...

Something fell on me from above. A hand covered my mouth. I struck out wildly as I was forced to the ground. My arms were pinned down and a savage face, burnt brown and unkempt with dark piercing eyes, was staring into mine.

"Gag him quickly and search the bag – there's gold here in his tunic."

I kicked out frantically. Someone grasped my legs in an iron hold and bound them swiftly with something. "A book!" came a contemptuous snort, "and not worth much! Not a pretty coloured page in the whole thing." There was a thud as the precious volume landed in the ditch, "Tools – those can be sold. No more money though." My arms were tied now and expert fingers were running over my person, searching for signs of more gold coins. There were none.

"Let's be off. Don't like this spot – road's too busy these days."

"Should we make an end of him first?"

"No, you fool! Why do you think we've tied him up? Can't risk our lives to the law for so little money and a few tools! It will be a good while before he's able to raise an alarm if we've done the job on him well. No, not in the ditch. No one will *ever* find him there, he'll be done for! Push him under the bushes – and let's away before anyone passes – I tell you I don't like the place."

Rough bare feet kicked me and horny hands dragged me deep into the bushes out of sight. Running footsteps, then silence but for a blackbird above me warning, "Pink, pink, pink, pink ... "

Trembling from head to foot so that my teeth seemed to rattle in spite of the gag, I listened. The blackbird's warning ceased and there was no human sound from the ancient high road. Morcant had once told me it had been made before my own Saxon kind ever came to Wessex. The forest seemed as empty now as it had been before the old inhabitants, the great ones who had conquered, subdued and ruled even Morcant's own wild Celtic people, built the road. The huge ruins of their stone houses and castles were still to be seen all over Wessex, sticking up like huge broken teeth out of the ground, the work of giants, the ignorant villagers said. Now their road was used by the fyrd, the trader, the traveller – and the robber. I tried to think clearly and escape from the fear that paralysed my mind. Think! There was a good chance that someone passing might not see me. Think! I would have to get the gag out of my mouth somehow to be sure of rescue. Thinking gave way to action and I began rubbing my head against the root of a tree.

The robbers had not meant me to die or they would have left me in the ditch but they had certainly given themselves a good start on anyone who might come to my aid. My squirming and struggling gradually produced results and the gag slipped down over my chin. My first instinct was to immediately call for help but I realised that was to risk having the robbers return to do a better job, if they were still within earshot. Better to wait until I could hear someone coming. But I wanted to shout! My whole terrified being was clamouring inside me for human help – how could I just lie there? Never before – or since – have I ever had to force my mind to master my feelings to such an extent. "Better to wait," my mind said firmly and with its aid I was somehow able to force my trembling body to remain silent.

It was not giants but the soldiers of the Roman Empire who had built the road. They had made it in the far-off days before the empire had earned the added title "Holy" that it bears in these Christian times. A pagan empire it was in those days, although I had heard tell that the first Christians ever to reach our shores were in the ranks of its army. But they had gone, those great ones, hundreds of years ago and we Saxons had taken their fertile land, pushing the Celts, whom the Roman Empire had ruled, ever westward, if they resisted us, into the wild and barren hills of Wales. Nowadays King Alfred found the great highways useful to enable his fyrdmen to move about quickly in response to the threat of attack or invasion from the Vikings. How I hoped to hear the sound of their steady march or perhaps one of their scouts running with a message now! I strained my ears, pushing down that terrible urge to shout by trying to get free from my bonds. But nothing I could do seemed to shift the knots around my feet or hands.

Then, at last, a faint noise of jingling harness met my ear. Could it be the fyrd? It certainly sounded like more than one horse. Now all my pent-up terrors were released in a great yell. "Help!" I shouted. Then again, "Help, help!"

When the astonished packhorse driver had pulled me out of the bushes and untied my wrists and ankles I do not know which of the two of us was the more terrified. I was still shaking violently and all he could say was, "We must get away from here quickly," over and over again.

"B...b...but the b...b...b...book!" I cried as well as my chattering teeth would allow. "I m...m...m...must find it!" As best as I could in my shocked state I explained what had happened and with the utmost reluctance he consented to help me grub about in the ditch until we recovered it, soiled and battered but otherwise unharmed. I must put his kindness on record for he went to the trouble, as one of his mares was only lightly laden, of quickly shifting her burden onto other horses and hoisting me and my book onto the pack-saddle. Then he started his train of animals and off we went, never slackening pace until the highway left the forest and came out into open fields surrounding a village. Here he was intending to stay the night.

# The Road

I had stopped shaking by this time but was quite unable to eat any of the cold bannock bread he offered me, though I drank a little water from his bottle. The staring eyes and wild face of the robber who had sprung on me kept coming back to me, making me shiver again.

"I can take you on with me tomorrow if you like," he offered, seeing the state I was in. "I have some business to do here today and I want to rest the horses."

"Where are you going?" I asked.

"I'm heading for a place called Leofham eventually, a few days west of here."

"Leofham!" I replied in thankful surprise, "that's my home! But why are you going there with your loaded animals? Leofham is a small place and out of the way for trade. What are you carrying?"

"Tin mostly," he said, "and some crockery and a few bits of imported jewellery that I picked up as a bargain – should sell well at Leofham!"

I stared at him, incredulous. There was no tinsmith at Leofham, and Frithestan, the village potter, made all our rough pots. As for jewellery, much as Leofham women may have wanted it, coin would be needed to pay for it and coin was a commodity Leofham did not have in abundant supply. But I did not feel equal yet to long conversation, only grateful that I could go home in safety with him, so I said, "Well, my friend, I am afraid I cannot reward you. All my little store of money was taken."

He mumbled something about being pleased to help and set about finding us lodgings in one of the village huts.

# Chapter 2
# Homecoming

It was just after midday when we arrived in the little village. The packhorse man was well known there as it was one of his regular stopping places. When he told my story there was sympathy and I did not lack for food, water and the offer of a bed, even though I could not pay for any of these things.

I was sitting on a bench, outside the hut where the packhorse man was staying, not long before nightfall, when another traveller, well mounted on a smart riding horse, also arrived in the village.

"Wulfgar!" he cried, as he dismounted gracefully, "We can travel together again at least a little further. I wondered if I would catch you up! Where are you staying?"

It was Brother Grifo looking pink, rather than green, and in excellent spirits! He had no guide with him and had obviously been enjoying his ride through the countryside.

"How do you come to be here?" I asked in surprise as he dismounted.

"I began to feel better not long after you left," he explained, "so much better that it was not long before I was able to eat a little food. That made me feel better still. That old woman you left me with found me a guide and a horse at a very reasonable price and we set off a couple of hours after you."

"Guide?" I asked looking round.

"Oh, I sent him home again after a while," said Brother Grifo. "He gave me plain directions and it seemed easy enough, the road was well made and clear. I was expecting to catch you up too, as you were on foot."

I was staggered. Brother Grifo had innocently ridden alone with no guide along the unfamiliar roads, presumably right past where I had been set upon, and now here he was, fresh as a daisy, politely asking whether anyone could provide him with supper!

"I'm very sorry I did not wait and come with you," I said, as he tucked into some good thick pottage. "It would have been better for me if I had!" and I explained to him what had happened to me.

At this he suddenly became much more thoughtful. "We must stick together from now on until our ways diverge," he said soberly, putting down his spoon, "I had not realised there was so much danger."

"To be fair, I think I was unlucky," I said. "Things are better than they used to be in Wessex when I was young. No road was safe then. The Viking raids left everywhere very lawless. I am travelling with the packhorse team I told you about, whose driver rescued me from the ditch and he has lent me a horse. I'm sure you could join us until we reach the place where the Æt Baðum road turns off northwards."

He eagerly agreed to my suggestion. It was a much more grave Brother Grifo who paid for his meal, courteously thanking our hosts for their kindness, and insisting on paying for my food and lodging too.

I did not sleep well that night although the little hut was comfortable enough and our hosts were kind. The robber's face haunted me as soon as I shut my eyes and I could hear the voice of his companion, "Should we make an end of him ...?" going round and round in my head. Then I began trembling again until I thought I would wake the whole house with the chattering of my teeth.

We all set off together at first light the next morning. Brother Grifo and I rode together behind the packhorses, chatting as we had done when walking across Francia, sometimes talking and sometimes companionably silent. I was glad to have his company again.

"Having seen a little of Wessex these last days of our journey, I begin to imagine now what a change it must have been for you when you arrived in Francia, if you had never been anywhere else before." he said, kindly. "Everything must have seemed so strange at first. Did it take long to adjust to our Frankish ways?"

"Oh yes," I replied. "At first the new environment was such a wrench from everything I knew and understood that, looking back, I think I struggled to survive at all. There were some similarities, of course, to Wessex. Corvey being on the very edge of Christendom helped."

Brother Grifo raised his eyebrows, "Really?"

"Yes, you see, to the north of Corvey are places where Christianity is struggling for survival, battered by Viking raids and conflicts. Then further north still are pagan lands, Denmark, Norway, Sweden. You know how Corvey sent, and is still sending, a stream of missionaries there and you know too how their work is often overthrown by rival chiefs or manoeuvring local kings as soon as their backs are turned. All this was something I could grasp because I was not unfamiliar with such circumstances myself."

"Ah, I understand," said Brother Grifo.

"I had come from a war-torn frontier of Christianity myself," I elaborated, "and I knew only too well from personal experience how quickly a veneer of half-understood Christian ideas could vanish and the old pagan ideas resurface. But there were other things that were so utterly foreign that at first I was in a state of confusion bordering on shock."

"For example?"

"Well," I paused trying to get my confused early impressions into some sort of order. Brother Grifo was a cultured man and I tried to match his way of speaking, "Well, at the Abbey itself with its magnificent buildings, its great library and beautiful music there was a scholarly calm, like the eye of a storm. Here I experienced a form of Christianity that was ... that was organised in a hierarchy, where decisions were referred up a chain that ended with the bishop of Rome, the Pope."

"This was new to you then?" Brother Grifo was surprised.

"Oh yes, I had heard of it dimly but never experienced it."

"And the other things that struck you as different?"

"Scholarship, for one thing. I had known only one scholar before. Morcant of Tyddewi, the Celt who had settled in our Saxon village and taught us from the Holy Scriptures. Morcant had only taught us to compare one part of Scripture with another to find out the plain meaning. That was all I knew."

Brother Grifo smiled gently at such endearing ignorance, "Ah yes, but then you discovered that we scholars knew this plain, literal meaning to be relatively unimportant. True scholars seek out the deeper, more significant meanings which we call the allegorical, the tropological, the anagogical. You, I suppose, had never heard of things with such long names."

"No, I hadn't and I'm afraid at first I reacted badly! I was inclined to be argumentative. How was it possible for the individual Christian to know the meaning of the Holy Scriptures if so much scholarship was needed? Even if he could read, he would be stuck at the plain, literal level and this would be of little use to him."

"Indeed," said Brother Girfo earnestly, "it might even lead him astray, for the literal sense clouds the true meaning. But, no doubt, there were always patient answers of one kind or another to your little questions."

"Oh yes, and gradually I began to settle down, fit in and lose my ignorant Wessex ways of thinking. As my skill increased, so did my confidence and with my confidence came the assurance that I should shed my old ideas and embrace those of the wise and cultured people around me."

"Do you think I will also have to adjust at Æt Baðum then?" said Brother Grifo and there was a slight tinge of anxiety in his voice.

"Well, you will find out that the roads and fields are not the only differences," I said.

"What do you mean?"

"Well, before I was sent to Francia, I had been assured I should to go to the Holy Books of Scripture for everything I needed to know; for a lattice through which to view the whole world. Now, I have found out that things are not that simple."

"The Scripture *is* the Word of God," he replied gravely, "and we should look to it to guide our behaviour."

"Ah, yes," I said, "that's quite correct, no one in Christendom would disagree with you, but at Corvey Abbey commentaries on the Scriptures – the glosses – and the writings of Popes like Gregory the Great and saints like Jerome or Augustine, the great Christian thinkers of the past, are all studied and diligently compared by learned scholars of the church. At Corvey they pour the writings of Scripture through this sieve of learning to clarify them."

"Indeed, a good metaphor," replied Brother Grifo. "The literal surface meaning is like a veil covering the spiritual sense of the words and the spiritual sense can only be understood by scholars."

"Exactly," I said, "but you won't find that attitude at Leofham where I come from and no doubt even at Æt Baðum there is not much of it! When I was young, Master Morcant merely translated the Scripture books into Anglo-Saxon for us. What else could he do in such a lonely outpost, to be fair? He taught us just to trust each of the Scripture books themselves to shed light on the others. It was not until I got to Corvey that I learned that it was naïve to think that ordinary peasants could be trusted to understand the Scripture for themselves. The church is strong and its priests and monks powerful at Corvey; in Leofham where I grew up it was just about clinging on to life. I adjusted my views and became more sophisticated at Corvey. After all, what is the point of coming to such a place to learn if you resolutely close your mind to what it has to teach you?"

"But now you will surely find things changed when you get home," said Brother Grifo encouragingly. "Your noble King Alfred has been encouraging learning throughout the land. These days there will be many clerks who understand the deep meaning of allegory, for instance, which is so much more important than just the literal words of Scripture."

"I hope so," I said doubtfully, "but you know, Wessex folk are stubborn. Once they have it in their heads that they can interpret Scripture for themselves, they won't take kindly to someone telling them they need a clerk to do it for them."

Brother Grifo sighed. "This is a problem elsewhere too," he admitted, "and yet it must be stopped. How is the Church to retain

# Homecoming

its power over the lay people if they think they can understand God's teaching for themselves?"

I was surprised. I had never heard it put in those terms so starkly before and it gave me a jolt. The Church officials keeping the Scriptures hidden from ordinary people in order to have power over them? How could that be right? I was quiet for a moment, puzzling over his words as if they were some kind of riddle. Was he mistaken? Brother Grifo noticed my silence and tactfully changed the subject.

"Have you any idea what Æt Baðum is like?" he asked politely. "I am guessing it is like the hot spring at Aachen in Middle Francia where it is not just the great baths themselves but the magnificent palace and cathedral that are famous all over Francia."

I did not really know how to answer this question as I had never been to Æt Baðum and had certainly never heard about any grand palace or huge cathedral there. I was non-committal, "Wessex is not like Francia," I repeated. "The Viking raids have made it difficult here."

He tutted sympathetically and then enlivened the next several miles with a description of a visit his father had made to Aachen as a child in the days when the great emperor Charlemagne ruled there in all his splendour.

The next day, our ways parted and Brother Grifo took the Æt Baðum road. He bade me a courteous farewell and I promised to look him up if I was ever in Æt Baðum. "And you'd be most welcome at Leofham," I added as I waved him goodbye.

I rode on after the packhorses, drinking in with a glad heart the clean smell of my native Wessex earth, newly turned by the plough, in the fallow fields. I thought with pleasure how much I would have to tell my old friends about what I had learned. But then the riddle came back to me and I remembered Brother Grifo's words about such people, "How is the Church to retain its power ... if they think they can understand God's teaching for themselves?" I had learned so much at the imposing imperial abbey-church-fortress at Corvey but before I went there I had assumed that I – and Eanflæde, and Swefred and the rest of my village friends – could understand God's Word for ourselves. What would they make of words like "tropological"? I searched my memory to recall what exactly "tropological" meant but found I was already forgetting – if I had ever fully understood. I tried to face the riddle squarely: were powerful, educated people like Brother Grifo using the peasants' ignorance of the deeper meanings of the Holy Books to keep their power over them? Another, even more chilling idea rose in my mind. Suppose the plain words of the Scripture *were* the most important thing? And suppose the powerful people would prefer that the peasants did not realise they *could* understand it themselves? I frowned, turning the riddle over in my mind. No, Brother Grifo, whatever his faults, was not a deceiver, not at that level. He believed what he had said. I was imagining things, drawing wrong conclusions. Better leave these things to those that understood them.

We halted to eat at a small village. The driver was unwilling to stop for long and on we pressed, riding side by side now the road was wider until we reached the spot where the old track leading to Leofham left the ancient road and dived once more towards the forest.

I could hardly recognise the place, once so familiar. The old track had been nothing more than a gap in the brambles: anyone who was not on the alert would pass without being aware of its existence. Not any more! A broad new road led off the old highway right in the direction of the village. "This is all new!" I exclaimed.

"You said you'd been away eight years or more," said the packhorse man. "The landscape has changed a lot in eight years –

## Homecoming

I should know, I travel all over Wessex! King Alfred is still battling with those evil Viking marauders. Some of them come as pirates from overseas and some are under that vicious traitor Guthrum or Athelstan or whatever he calls himself. They could pour in from north and east of Wessex at any moment. New roads are part of the king's plan to defeat them."

"Even before I had left, the king had begun fortifying Wessex and linking up the forts with better roads," I said. "Our Thane Pelhere never trusted Guthrum and he was right! Guthrum swore peace with King Alfred after the Battle of Edington but he broke his oath. I heard about a sea battle while I was away; news of that reached even Corvey."

"Oh, you heard about that, did you? A famous victory and no mistake! Alfred and his men finished off a load of pirate Vikings – all killed or captured they were. Did you hear about Ebbisham?"

"What happened there?" I asked, hoping it was Viking defeat and not a reverse for the king.

"That was Guthrum's lot again," said the packhorse man, "right inside Wessex itself! But the king and the fyrd drove them out. And then there were raids and counter-raids all that year. Rochester, Benfleet and then the king took his troops right into the Danelaw. All fighting alongside each other they were, the pirate Vikings and Gutham's lot." He spat contemptuously, "Mind you, they quarrelled among themselves sometimes, all the different tribes of 'em, and then the pirates would go off home! Did you not get much news from home then?"

"I heard nothing for ages! I was beginning to wonder if Wessex still existed! Then I heard from some monks that the king had occupied some town or other – on the great river which divides Guthrum's Danelaw from Wessex and Mercia."

"Oh, that's London," he said. "The king drove out the Vikings

29

Wulfgar and the Riddle

from there and then fortified the place – built a good new bridge too. Then he put Ealdorman Æthelred of Mercia in charge of the place."

"I have heard nothing from Leofham itself for more than a year," I said. "Do you think the king's new fortifications mean we'll have peace in Wessex in the end?"

But now we were deep in the forest again and the packhorse man became silent and anxious again, merely grunting in reply and urging his team on at a brisker pace. In my childhood there had been no robbers anywhere near Leofham but things might be different now. He was keen to get there before darkness but the dusk was beginning to fall when at last I made out something of the familiar outline of the village ahead of us.

"Nearly there!" I exclaimed in happy excitement. "Look!"

"That's right," he said much more cheerfully, "not far now!" and then, to my amazement, the new road lurched to the right leaving only the rough remains of the old track leading towards the village.

"Hey!" I shouted, reigning in my horse as he plunged off down the new road, his tired team plodding wearily after him. "Where are you off to? There's the village ahead of us!"

"No, no," he shouted back, "that's the *old* village – no one there now – follow me!" and he rode on in front with his team.

For a moment I hesitated and then, puzzled and distressed, I turned my horse after the pack animals and down the smart new road towards the river.

A massive wooden gatehouse with a sentry, a wide timber bridge, another gate, another sentry. This was not the homecoming I had longed for; it was another world. Dazed, I followed the last of the pack horses up a broad empty street, a complete stranger in an unknown town.

I reined in my horse for a moment, hoping for some familiar face but there seemed to be no one about. But then, as I squinted round my unfamiliar surroundings in the gathering dusk trying to get some sort of bearings, I heard a piping voice calling, "chicky, chicky, chicky ... " as though to gather in some hens for the night. I prepared to follow the pack horses as they plodded up the road when a child appeared round the corner of one of the little houses, still calling. At the same time a flurry of assorted chickens scuttered in her direction from somewhere out of the gloom and ran flapping and clucking towards her right under my horse.

"Hey you," I called, as my tired mount thought for an instant about rearing and then decided it would all be too much effort and settled for a sort of sideways cavort instead, "watch what you are doing with those hens!"

A little white face appeared. "Sorry, Sir, didn't see you, Sir."

I peered down at the girl whose face had a slightly familiar look that I could not place. The pack horses had disappeared round a corner but I supposed, now I was inside the town, I could easily find them again. "Can you direct me to the house of Morcant, the Celt?" I asked, patting the neck of the disgruntled horse and hoping that my dear old friend Morcant had not disappeared along with every other familiar thing.

"Oh, yes, Sir, he's my father, Sir. Just come this way, Sir," and, tucking a crooning hen under each arm, she led the way back round the corner whence she had appeared, still chicky-chickying away to the rest of her flock as they straggled after her.

A woman's figure blocked the firelight at the doorway of one of the little low houses for a moment and then she stepped briskly outside wiping her hands on her apron and calling, "Edeva, get those hens in quickly now – it's dark already."

My new acquaintance hurried up all apologies again, "Sorry, Mother, the little one would not come at first and then they all startled this traveller's poor horse – he's looking for Father, is he in?"

The figure stepped quickly towards us and I could see the competent set of her shoulders. The keys and spindle hanging from her girdle were outlined in the dancing light from the doorway. I knew who it must be.

"Traveller? horse?" Eanflæde, wife of Morcant, was staring up at me now, "Who ... not Wulfgar! Is it? Yes it is! – Morcant, Swefred, it's Wulfgar! Boys! come quickly and see to the horse!"

At last I *was* home.

# Chapter 3
# Leofham Burgh

Morcant and Eanflæde's little home was overflowing with children as ever. Every nook and cranny seemed full of them, some already sleeping, some wide-eyed and eager to meet their visitor and the older boys swarming out to look after the horse.

"Wulfgar!" boomed a voice and a long-legged, gangly man with a straggling beard unwound himself yard after yard from a pile of dogs in a corner, "Is it really you?" and Swefred was throwing long arms round me and thumping me on the back.

"Run and fetch your father, quickly, some of you," Eanflæde was saying. "He must be still up at the church – girls put the pot on! Master Wulfgar must be famished! Boys, that horse needs taking to the fyrd stables!"

By the time Morcant arrived, the whole household was awake and I was being sat down to a meal of the familiar Wessex pottage like a guest of honour at a royal feast. And now I was really hungry and could eat everything Eanflæde put in front of me. Everyone was answering my questions at once and asking their own so it was a while before I was able to explain that I had been set upon and robbed on the road. With so many little pairs of ears taking in my news I made light of the whole affair not wishing to spoil the joyful occasion or to be responsible for nightmares. Besides, here in the warmth of home the whole episode seemed so distant and somehow unreal that I wanted to dismiss it from my thoughts altogether lest it haunt me too. I soaked up the familiar

## Wulfgar and the Riddle

surroundings: the house might be different, the village might have changed but Eanflæde's spindle twirled and dropped with the new spun yarn, just as it had always done. The same comfortable and comforting atmosphere enclosed me; this was home.

And yet as we talked, things were not *quite* the same. The experience of the robbery had knocked some of my new-found self-confidence a bit but I still found Morcant horribly parochial after listening to him for just five minutes. The Bible this, the Scripture that, the Holy Books the other! How did he presume to know what everything in the Bible meant? All he knew was the plain meaning of the words in front of him! He had no commentaries, no patristic writings to refer to, no scholars to consult with; who was he to talk about how one should worship or what it means to pray? Morcant obviously had as much to learn as I had had when I left home eight years ago! I thought of the riddle that had bothered me earlier and felt inclined to agree with Brother Grifo. Carefully, I explained to Morcant what I'd been told about the literal sense of the Word of God being less important than the spiritual sense but he was sceptical.

"But where do you find such a strange idea in the Word itself?" he asked in his nitpicking way, "and what of the Holy Spirit, whom God sends to illuminate *all* his children?"

When he got round to asking me what I'd been doing in Francia, I seized the opportunity with both hands.

"Well, I've improved my carving; it's really good now," I said proudly. "You should see what I can do! Makes the dragon's head I did before I went away look amateurish! I've done panels, fancy screens and you should see my figure carving! You see, the common people need something solid they can see to help them in their worship. They need the cross before their eyes; they need to picture the gospel stories – especially if they cannot read." This had been a new revelation to me in Francia for no one in Leofham had ever made any mention of such a thing.

I suppose I should have guessed the response!

"Hmm ... Where do you find this idea in Scripture?" asked Morcant, repeating his favourite phrase.

"You will have to get rid of this idea that *everything* is just spelled out plainly in the Scripture," I said impatiently. "Scripture is dark and difficult to interpret. In Francia they realise that to understand it scholars need the light of the traditions of the Church, especially the written wisdom of the Church fathers. The meaning of the Scripture is not just in the plain words on the page for any ignoramus to read."

Eanflæde's yarn broke suddenly. "God's Word is not dark," she said, winding off the new spun yarn. "It is very light itself." Her spindle twirled and dropped again, and there was silence.

Next morning, Morcant was off to see the thane about the robbery before I had even shaken myself awake. I had not slept well. The comforts of home could not prevent the experiences I had gone through on the road from taking effect and, try as I might, the gaunt face of the robber still kept appearing as soon as I closed my eyes. Every detail of his wild hair and sunburnt skin was clear as day and his wild eyes drilled into me. I tossed and turned on the straw pallet. If I opened my eyes, I began to worry. How could I work without tools, how could I replace the tools without money and how could I earn money without work? If I closed my eyes there was that terrible face ... At last a troubled and restless sleep had claimed me.

"Morcant says he'll be back later," explained Eanflæde, "and the boys have returned that packhorse to the driver. I expect the thane will want a full report from you sometime today but in the meantime Swefred will take you to the church and show you everything. Things have certainly improved since you went away! The Vikings would have a job to raid Leofham Burgh as they planned to raid the old village!"

## Wulfgar and the Riddle

"They did not get away with it even then!" I said, remembering the events of that terrible night and reflecting, even as I said it, that some of us in Leofham had paid a high price for freedom.

We were standing at the low doorway of Eanflæde and Morcant's new home and now that the sun was up I could see more of my unfamiliar surroundings. "Come on!" said Swefred, appearing from nowhere with a couple of hounds at his heels, "I'll take you up the church tower; you'll see it all from there," and he strode on ahead of me whistling to his dogs.

"He's grown tall enough to see everything without going up a tower!" I said to Eanflæde as I prepared to follow him.

She nodded, quietly proud of her eldest son. "A good boy," she said softly, "and just like his father," and she turned back into the darkened doorway.

I followed Swefred and the dogs down one of the four roads that met in the centre of the Burgh. Beside the crossroads was a timber church with a stone tower. Stone towers are something of a novelty in Wessex. We Anglo-Saxons are not anything like as skilled as stone masons as the Franks and we prefer to build in wood. I was curious to see this church tower at close quarters.

"The stone came in by river," explained Swefred. "I went with the boats that fetched it. You should have seen the place, Wulfgar – not far up river from here – a huge wreck of a building – made by giants, someone told me, in days gone by! Great walls and parts of towers sticking up out of the ground there were. All the builders had to do was sort and grade the stone when we got it back here; the old giant people had already cut it and shaped it."

I smiled, knowing more of what this ruin might have been and who its builders were than Swefred, although there was a time when I would have been as untaught as he. Now I knew much more about history and who had ruled and guarded Wessex long before we Anglo-Saxons had come. But there was no point in trying to explain to Swefred, I thought smugly. He had grown up in an environment of ignorance.

But even with its ready-shaped stones, Leofham church tower was not in the least like the westwerk of Corvey Abbey, under whose shadow I had lived for the last few years. Close up, the tower seemed rough, although sturdy. Swefred tied up the dogs and showed me inside. "Plenty of space for refuge in an emergency," he explained proudly. "Cattle can be driven in here if needed too." And he led the way up the steep winding stair, calling out as he did so, "Ho, sentry! It's only me, Swefred, with a visitor!"

Sure enough, when we emerged onto the roof there was the sentry, pacing round and round inside the parapet, his signal horn hanging at his waist and a huge pile of brushwood ready for his beacon should it be needed. Clearly no Vikings would ever be able to make a surprise attack on Leofhan now.

From the tower I could see that, compared to the old village, Leofham Burgh was extensive. Inside secure walls punctuated with watchtowers were houses, each with its own kale-yard, running off the long main street. Everything was laid out in straight lines in a grid pattern and there were streets of houses and shops as well as an empty quarter which, as Swefred explained, could be occupied at a moment's notice by the fyrd. He pointed out his own home and I could see the little house in a line that looked like tiny beeskeps from this distance. Beyond was fallow ground, where the ploughman was already hard at work. The cry of "*Gāþ! gāþ!* Walk-on, walk-on!" from the ox-goader, rose faintly on the morning air and from my vantage point I could see the dip and swoop of gulls searching for good things turned over by the plough. Opposite the church was the thane's new hall. Two small figures – the thane and Morcant – were visible standing outside the entrance, deep in conversation.

I could have gazed at the morning landscape for hours but Swefred was eager to show me round the inside of the little church. This turned out to be absolutely plain, its timber walls made of huge split logs, smoothed inside with an adze but quite rough looking on the outside. "Couldn't you do better than this for the church, Swefred?" I asked. "It's not much more than a hut!" This was not quite true and I was forgetting that when I left Leofham there had been no church building at all. But I was struck by the contrast between the mighty building I had been working on at Corvey, with its beautiful carvings and decorations, and this humble construction which was the church of my native folk. The conversation of the previous night had nettled me too and I was not tactful.

Swefred looked a bit crestfallen. "We did our best," he mumbled, "and Morcant said we should keep it plain and simple – no distractions."

That afternoon, Morcant, Eanflæde and I sat inside the doorway of their new home. The children were outside playing in the thin April sun and the house was quiet.

"The thane wants you to make a report today," said Morcant. "He keeps a record of this kind of thing – robbers and so on – and despatches will go to various burghs via the fyrd. Did you lose anything that could be easily identified?"

"Yes," I said at once, "all my tools! They are marked. I have carved my initials on the handles. The two letters W W but with the second W upside down above the first so that it looks like a double diamond or a pair of lozenge shapes." In the comfortable light of day the cycle of no tools, no work; no work, no money; no money, no tools seemed less unbreakable than it had done the night before. After all, the king had summoned me back. If he had a job for me, tools would be provided. I turned to something else that was bothering me. Why had I had no letter from Morcant for over a year? When I mentioned this, Morcant was surprised.

"Did you not get the one I wrote about this time last year?" he asked. "Telling all about the proposals for the new Burgh?"

I shook my head. "For all I knew," I said with a smile, "you could have left Wessex altogether and gone back to your old lord, Prince Hyfaidd, in Wales!"

Morcant laughed, "It's funny you should say that, Wulfgar, because if everything goes according to plan, I may be meeting again with the ruler of my native Dyfed, although I will not have to go back to Wales to do so."

"What do you mean?" I asked, "He's not coming here, surely!"

"Not here, no," explained Morcant, "but Prince Hyfaidd is coming to a town on the border of Mercia and Wessex in order to acknowledge King Alfred as his overlord. You see, his enemies have got him with his back to the wall in Dyfed and he wants King Alfred's overlordship to give him some protection."

"But you can't go, can you? I mean, you are not allowed to leave Leofham."

"No, that's quite right," said Morcant, "I would still be over there in the ruins of the old village all on my own if the king had not given me permission to come here! The king has his reasons for keeping me out of the way as a rule but on this occasion he wants my presence. Apart from anything else, the prince is my countryman and I speak his native language. I will be useful and so the king has summoned me."

"Will he end his prohibition completely, do you think?" I asked, trying to ignore the rather gloomy way Morcant seemed to be looking at the king's actions. "Or will you have to return here afterwards under the same conditions as before?"

"I'm not sure," said Morcant. "The king is a most gracious

## Wulfgar and the Riddle

sovereign and I am honoured when he calls on me for counsel. He has visited Leofham Burgh with the fyrd and sometimes when we talk of the Holy Books of Scripture and read them together I see his mind swaying towards a complete dependence only on the plain words of those books. And yet always, just when I think he is breaking away from the bonds that hold him, he draws back. I sometimes fear that he keeps me here because he is afraid (and it's a ridiculous idea, for what could one ignorant old clerk do in any case?) that I would somehow be able to spread the ideas he longs for and yet fears all over Wessex."

"The king is a wise man," I said trying to be diplomatic in response to what seemed (to someone who had been to Francia) rather silly remarks, "and I'm sure he would like to have you by his side more often."

"We'll see," said Morcant. Then, "I wrote to you about the church building too; did you not get that letter either?"

"No, nothing," I said. "I had no idea of what has been going on in Leofham – Leofham Burgh that is. It's very ... well ... plain, the church ... isn't it?" I tried to be tactful after our last conversation but I must have overdone the tact for, to my surprise, Morcant seemed to take my remarks as a compliment.

"Oh yes," he said enthusiastically, "no distractions. We can hold our services there just as simply as we did in the old days before we had a church building at all."

"It's certainly different from the building I've been working on," I said. "You should see it, Morcant, and more than that, you should hear it! The construction has a wonderful effect on the voices of the singers. Even a single voice swoops and soars and fills the space so beautifully."

"Well, I'm sure we have no need of that at Leofham Burgh," laughed Morcant. "We are rather rough and ready in our singing,

I'm afraid, but then we are pouring out our hearts to God in his praise and it is our hearts he is hearing, not our voices."

For a moment I felt as if there was the faintest of rebukes in his words and I hesitated, glancing at his cheerful, round face. No, there was no criticism in his eyes; any rebuke I felt must have come from my own imagination.

"I've brought you a book," I said, changing the subject again."The robbers threw it into the ditch but the packhorse man and I managed to get it out. It has not come to much harm."

"A book?" said Morcant. "That's a lavish gift, Wulfgar!"

"Yes, but it's not from me," I explained.

"Now I really am curious!" said Morcant. "Who would send me a book?"

Even at Corvey Abbey, it was not absolutely everyone who favoured long and complex explanations and discussions above the plain words of Scripture. I came across one man even in that sophisticated place, who had the same primitive ideas as Morcant. Brother Mariwig was a very odd character and the present was from him.

"It's from one of the monks at Corvey Abbey, Mariwig his name is, he works in the scriptorium – a strange fellow," I said in answer to Morcant's question, "a bit of a loner, in fact, with ideas of his own. When he heard me telling the monks about you and how you arrived at our village and told us all the gospel, he was fascinated. After that he often asked me about you. I think it was the way you taught the villagers just by reading them the Holy Scriptures that appealed to him."

I paused, remembering the odd little monk with the long nose and limping gait. Unpopular with the others, he had returned to monastic life after some illness or injury had forced him to abandon his missionary calling to some far northern place among the Swedes. He had never really settled back into the monastery and was always raising awkward, and it seemed to me then unnecessary, questions. He never quoted Jerome or Gregory or other old writers about the Scriptures and was constantly pointing out places where their commentaries contradicted what the Scriptures said elsewhere or where the allegories the commentators drew from the text of Scripture seemed to him ridiculous.

"Go on," said Morcant interested, "why did he send me a book?"

"He copied it for you himself," I said, "because – now let me get this right – he thinks there are some ideas around nowadays about how we view the bread and wine in church which run counter to the plain teaching of the Scriptures. No one else agrees with him, of course, but he got the idea, from what I told him about you, that you might be different – I don't quite understand why. I'll go and get it for you, I put it by my bed place."

"Your friend may have a point, but I prefer to get my teaching from the books of the Holy Scriptures themselves, not other books," said Morcant, ever a man of one idea. "The trouble is nowadays no one seems to read the Scriptures and just listen to the plain meaning of the words."

"That's exactly what Mariwig would say himself," I replied, and I thought, as I rummaged among the bedding, of Brother Grifo and his riddling remark, "but, personally, I can't believe the whole church is wrong altogether." I did not add, "and only you and Mariwig are right," but I thought it. "Here it is," and I handed him the fat little volume. "He told me, if I remember rightly, that it's a treatise by someone from Corbie Abbey. It was monks from Corbie Abbey that founded the Abbey at Corvey originally. He's also copied some correspondence between an old Bishop – of

Turin, I think he said – and someone or other. He's written a note for you at the beginning anyway so you'll get the picture."

Morcant slid open the shutter of the window by his reading desk, letting in a shaft of pale light that seemed almost blue with the dancing specks and motes of dust which coloured it. He took the little book from me, laid it on the desk and carefully opened the plain leather front cover. For a while there was silence. Morcant bent over his gift and nothing moved in the warm sunlight except Eanflæde's twirling spindle and dropping yarn.

When at last he raised his head there was a curious look in his eye. "This book looks interesting!" he said in a tone of surprise. "The books I read in the monastery at Tyddewi often left me frustrated but I feel this is going to be different."

"What do you mean, frustrated?" I asked.

"Well, the glosses, for instance, with their endless allegorical, anagogical and tropological interpretations (just long words for disregarding the plain meaning!); most of the time they seemed like a veil of smoke hanging over the Scripture that had to be penetrated before you could get to the truth itself," said Morcant, "but this is nothing like that."

This seemed all back to front to me but I persevered, "What is the book about?" I asked, "and was I right about the letter from Mariwig?"

"Yes," said Morcant, "there's a letter from him to me at the beginning. He writes good Latin. He says:

'To Morcant of Tyddewi, greetings from Mariwig, lately of Fröjel, now of Corvey Abbey. I have heard about you from your dear son in the faith, Wulfgar Waelwulfson, and take the liberty of sending with him this book for you. In it I have copied the treatise *Concerning the Body and Blood of the Lord* by Ratramnus of Corbie who died about 20 years ago. This was written at the request of the late Emperor Charles the Bald who visited Corbie in the year of Our Lord 843. It is a clear explanation of why teachings on this topic which are now so popular are in fact sadly wrong. His demonstration from the plain reading of the Scripture that the bread and wine physically remain just that (bread and wine) at the Lord's Supper has never been condemned by any authority of the church since his day. This is despite the fact that, in these present ignorant and superstitious days, it is everywhere being taught that the bread and wine changes into actual flesh and blood. I have also copied, after the treatise, a letter on a different but related subject (the idolatrous worship of images) from one Claudius, who was Bishop of Turin some 60 years ago, to his friend Theodemir, Abbot of Psalmody Monastery in the Languedoc. I find few, if any, around me who accept the teaching of these good men, since nowadays men blind their eyes to the truth of Scripture, diluting its authority by always viewing it through, as it were, the darkened glass of glosses or commentaries and their own endless allegories. What Wulfgar tells me of you makes me think you are of a different mind. Farewell.'"

"Doesn't mince his words, does he?" I said, reminded of Mariwig's blunt and grumpy manner and his resolute condemnation of all contemporary ideas as plain wrong just because they were built on a more sophisticated view of Holy Scripture than his own.

"No," replied Morcant, with a worryingly satisfied look, "he doesn't and I think I shall profit from what he has sent me. I'll write him a letter of thanks – though if your experience with letters from me is anything to go by, he won't get it!"

# Chapter 4
# Old Friends and a New Job

While Morcant read his new book, I went for a walk around the new Burgh. Swefred was off on some dog-related jaunt so I had be content with young Edeva as a guide. It was a rather depressing experience. In the years I had been away it was not just the buildings that had changed. This person had died, that had gone away, another had been killed fighting the Vikings while serving in the fyrd. Edeva, born after I left for Francia, had never heard of half the people I asked after. She chatted away cheerfully about her own friends who meant nothing to me. Had I really lost most of my old companions as well as my tools? I was beginning to wonder if I would have been better off if the king had allowed me to stay in Francia, when a big old one-armed fellow with a walking stick hobbled round the corner.

"Wulfgar!" he exclaimed joyfully. "They told me you were back! Welcome home."

I stared, not recognising this wreck of a man as anyone I had known.

"I'm Guthra!" he said. "You remember me, don't you?"

Guthra! The lad who always beat me at tree climbing! It could not be – strong, agile, youthful – reduced to this! The horror must have shown on my face for he looked down and mumbled, "Not what I was, I suppose. Lucky to be alive really after ... I was serving in the fyrd when the Vikings raided Rochester". He looked up at me now, "They ran away to their ships in the end but we gave them some good punishment before they got off."

"Excellent! I'm sure you gave them something to think about!" I exclaimed, pulling myself together with an effort. "We had reports in Francia that some Viking raids were taking place over in Kent but, of course, you only get muddled rumours and so on when you are so far away, not hard facts. All this," I waved my arms at the burgh, "is going to make it impossible for them now!"

"And have you seen the church?" asked Guthra proudly. "We've got a building to worship in now, you know, and I helped to put it up! I'm not finished yet; I can do quite a lot with my one arm if I have a bit of help here and there." He drew himself up straight, "Guthra, the one-armed stone mason, at your service!"

I felt suddenly lost for words at this shocking encounter but Edeva unintentionally came to my rescue. "I'm glad we saw you," she said to Guthra, "Father was asking after you yesterday about something needing doing to the tower and I was supposed to go and find you but I forgot! Could you call in and see him, please?"

"I'm going that way later on," said Guthra, "so I'll call in with pleasure. I'll see you later too, Wulfgar – good to have you home," and he hobbled slowly off in the direction of the church.

Edeva chattered on but I fell silent. Now that I *had* finally met someone from the old days I almost wished I had not. I was grateful when we rounded a corner and found ourselves back in the street where we had started.

"So now you've seen it all," she said, "and it's time for dinner!"

Dinner was the usual noisy affair but, when it was over, Morcant motioned me over to his reading desk.

## Old Friends and a New Job

"I take back my words," said Morcant. "Books other than the Scriptures themselves do have *some* value! At least they do when they point out the value of the Scripture! This one from your friend Mariwig is like an answer to prayer."

I was pleased to find Morcant was capable of changing his mind about something but I was concerned too. I knew the monks of Corvey regarded Mariwig as someone with unorthodox ideas that bordered on the heretical. Had I been unwise in agreeing to take Mariwig's gift to Morcant?

"What's in this book then?" I asked, slightly anxious. "I'm not sure you should take everything old Mariwig sent you as accurate; he's a bit of a funny character, you know."

"There are two different things in it," replied Morcant, "both reliable: the stories of how two other churchmen in the recent past have compared the practices of the church around them with the plain narrative of Scripture and found – um, certain differences. Their experience is so like my own that ... well it's encouraging."

"You mean they threw away all the writings of the past, all the traditions of holy church ..." I began, exasperated – and then I stopped myself. This was no way to talk, riddle or no riddle. Morcant was not only my senior but he had also been my dearest friend in a time of great loneliness and need; he deserved more respect and gentleness from me.

"I'm sorry, Morcant," I said. "I should be more respectful. What do these old writers say?"

"Ratramnus of Corbie – he is the more recent of the two – writes about the Lord's Supper as we read of it in Scripture," said Morcant, completely ignoring my little outburst. "He shows *from the Scriptures* that it is a memorial feast and the bread and wine are Christ's true body and blood but in a *symbolic* form. I this find a great comfort. It troubles me when I hear of those who make it

47

into something like pagan magic and tell the poor people they have changed bread and wine into Christ's actual body and blood and even that they should worship it. I, like Ratramnus, cannot find any justification for this idea in the Scriptures."

"And the second writer?" I asked, cautiously.

"Your friend Mariwig copied into this book the letter Claudius of Turin wrote not long after he had become a bishop. The letter was addressed to his friend and former colleague, Abbot Theodemirus, and he explains some of the troubles he had when he arrived in Turin. And again, it is wonderfully encouraging."

"What troubles?" I asked feeling rather lost as to how the difficulties of a bishop in Turin over sixty years ago could be an encouragement here and now in Leofham Burgh.

"The Emperor Louis the Pious had sent Claudius from Francia to be bishop in Turin and he says that when he arrived he was horrified to find that in every church and all over the city there were statues, images and crosses."

I opened my mouth to speak but Morcant swept on, "He writes that the people were addicted to bowing to them and reverencing them just as if they were idols – which of course they were. From this letter Claudius seems to have been something of a man of action. He did not waste any time arguing. He removed the whole lot – some of them with his own hands. Naturally the people were not pleased, at least at first, and he writes about a great deal of opposition. But he was determined to stick to his course. He was someone who had taken the trouble to consider what the Holy Scripture *actually says* about something that has also been worrying me. I am not alone!"

"But Morcant," I said, "this is thinking with some strange twists in it. A work of art is not an idol, it is just there to help people, especially people who can't read, to know something about their religion. Crosses, crucifixes, they are there to remind us of what happened ... the poor people ... how will they understand without it?"

"So why do people bow to them? Why do they kneel before them?" Morcant's tone was earnest.

"They are not worshipping the image itself, Morcant, they are worshipping the Lord depicted in the image."

"Wulfgar, Wulfgar, don't you see? What thinking pagan bowing before a statue of Tiw or Woden – or even a sacred tree – thinks he is worshipping the statue or tree itself? No! He is worshipping the god represented by the image or tree. There is no difference! And God, in the Scriptures, has declared plainly that this is not how he would be worshipped. Why, you only have to read the ten commandments given to Moses. And as for the cross, as Claudius pointed out, we are told by the Lord himself to *take it up* not bow down to it – by which the Lord signifies the bearing of tribulation as he bore the cross for us. It is not some magic talisman to ward off evil."

I confess I was appalled. It could not be that all my new-found sophistication was just an error. I had become so used, during my time at Corvey, to seeing everyone from the Abbot downwards turning and bowing to the figure of Christ on the cross. The poor people in the street inclined their heads towards the market cross or a wayside shrine or made the sign of the cross when danger threatened. Was this wrong, then? If so, and here a chill struck my heart, what I had been soaking up was heresy. But no! How could it be that most of the church was heretical? For a moment Brother Grifo's strange remark that had so bothered me came back to my mind. Here was the answer to the riddle then, surely. It was a ridiculous idea that Morcant, Mariwig and a few others could be right and everyone, *everyone*, else wrong, whatever Brother Grifo had meant by what he said.

Wulfgar and the Riddle

I was trying to put all this into words when there was a sudden scuffle. A lean old sow, tired no doubt of struggling to find anything worth eating outside, barged in through the open doorway. Eanflæde jumped up, flapping her skirts and giving chase but the old lady could obviously smell something more tasty inside than out and was reluctant to leave. "Wherever is Hrypa?" asked Eanflæde in exasperation. "What is he doing letting his animals roam around inside other people's houses?"

Our combined efforts failed to move the unwelcome visitor and we were glad when the ancient Hrypa hobbled into view calling, "Hup, hup, hup, here pig ..." to his straying charge.

"Hey, Hrypa! In here!" shouted Eanflæde. "One of your sows is rooting up my house-floor!"

It was quite a while before order was restored and Hrypa, as lean and old-looking as the sow herself, shooed her firmly outside and then planted himself in the doorway, his tattered tunic, the same colour as her bristles, flapping gently in the spring breeze. "Not much for her outside yet," he said by way of apology. "She's been rooting over the fallow but that's under plough now."

I had not been enjoying the conversation with Morcant. I felt glad of an interruption that would change the subject. But Morcant was not put off. "Hrypa," he said, returning serenely to the topic previously under discussion, "just the person to give us an opinion. What do you think from your understanding of the Holy Scripture? What should be our attitude to the cross of Christ?"

There was a long pause. It took Hrypa a little while to gather his thoughts. At last he said slowly, "Well, masters, it was a terrible thing. When I think of our dear Saviour dying there for me it makes me sorry I'm so sinful, masters, and that's a fact."

"And would you," continued Morcant, "bow to an image of the cross, or make a sign of the cross to help you in need?"

## Old Friends and a New Job

"Why should I do such things?" asked Hrypa and he seemed surprised. "As to the first thing you mentioned, I shall bow to my living Saviour one day in the very glory of heaven but not to a piece of wood or stone like a old pagan, and as for help in trouble, surely I should pray to my heavenly Father for that – aye, I have done many a time in Christ's name and the help never has failed."

I knew why Morcant had questioned Hrypa in this way, of course. He was well known in the village when I was younger as someone who had been utterly unable to learn to read despite genuinely wanting to do so. His answer was intended to demonstrate to me that the poorest and most ignorant were capable of understanding the gospel without the aid of crosses and statues. Again in my head I heard Brother Grifo's voice, "How is the church to retain its power ... if they think they can understand God's teaching for themselves?" I dismissed the remark as a riddle with no answer: I was being oversensitive. I told myself that Morcant had been my first teacher but now our paths had seriously diverged. I respected him, of course, but it followed that one of us must be moving in the direction of heresy. I knew which one of us that would be in the opinion of most of Christendom and it was not, could not be, me. But what about the opinion of God himself? I put away the thought as soon as it arose in my mind. No! How could that differ from the opinion of almost everyone in Christendom? The idea was ridiculous! It couldn't. Could it? Could it ... ?

It was later in the day that I knelt before the thane – and good old Thane Pelhere graciously bade me rise for all the world as though I had never been sent away in disgrace.

"A bad business this robbery on the road!" he exclaimed. "I gather from Morcant that you've lost not only your money but your tools. Morcant told me they were marked with a double lozenge symbol so if they turn up in a market somewhere we may recover them. I'm afraid I don't hold out much hope though, unless the robber himself is captured. If anyone is caught with

## Wulfgar and the Riddle

your tools on him, we'll know who we've got! However, as it turns out your tools are less of a loss to you than you imagine. I have instructions from the king, Wulfgar. You are to proceed at once to Shaftesbury!"

"Shaftesbury?" I had never even heard of the place. "Where is that? Why ... ?"

"The king is establishing an abbey there," explained the thane, "and has installed his daughter, Æthelgifu, as Abbess. She wished to retire to an abbey partly because her health is not good. Something of her father's old sickness she has but much worse, I understand. Even frankincense does her no good – not like the king. Shaftesbury is a healthy place with wonderful air. The king hopes it will help her. The abbey is fully functioning now and the builders have just completed the construction of the abbey chapel. I gather the king wants some wood carving to beautify the chapel before it is considered completely finished and he thought of you for the job. The reports of you he has had from Abbot Bovo have been excellent – and I'm not surprised! Everyone who sees that dragon head you carved for me before you went away thinks it is the most remarkable and lifelike thing they have ever seen! Here is the king's sealed letter to the Abbess for you to take with you and I'll detail a fyrdman to show you the way. Since you are on a commission from the king I have authority to provide you with whatever you need to do the job so there is a set of tools for you on its way from the smith today. You can set out tomorrow."

I should have slept soundly that night, or at least it should only have been excited anticipation of my new job that kept me awake. But I was still turning the riddle over in my mind. When I was young we had had little contact with the Christian Church. I was a poor ignorant peasant like those around me and we had no understanding of church teachings. In consequence when the clerks arrived from time to time to collect their *church-scott* (as their payments in money or food are called) their crosses seemed little different from the pagan religious symbols they were supposed to supplant and the bread and wine they sacrificed seemed to be just a version of the old sacrifices to Woden and Thor. As for the prayers in Latin that they intoned, they were like a charm recited in a magic language.

Then Morcant had arrived in Leofham and had taught us simply from the Scriptures about the God of creation, the sin and guilt of all mankind and the coming of the Saviour to die for sinners. This simple Scripture teaching seemed totally different to the activities of the clerks but by then Leofham had become cut off from all that by the Viking invasion in any case. We had the Scriptures; that was enough just then. We just deduced that there must be something quite wrong with the official church.

But now I had been living right at the heart of that church. The crosses, the Latin prayers, the beautiful singing inside beautiful buildings; now I could appreciate them. I could not explain all this to Morcant or expound the riddle to him. In Francia the peasants just looked on at everything with open-mouthed admiration, going through whatever motions they were taught by their betters for the good of their souls. Things here in Wessex, well, in Leofham Burgh at any rate, seemed to be different. Morcant and his peasants were not interested in looking on at higher things, they wanted to stay at the plain Scripture level. Were they just too stubborn to be taught anything better?

# Chapter 5
# The Riddling Nun

I set out for Shaftesbury accompanied by a rather surly and quiet fyrdman. As we rode through the dappled spring sunshine I tried to concentrate on the pleasant thought of meeting members of the Abbess Æthelgifu's new foundation. A new Benedictine Abbey directly patronised by the king would be exactly the place for me to exercise my skills unhindered by the quaint ideas of someone like Morcant with his strange fancies.

"How is the church to retain its power ... if they think they can understand God's teaching for themselves?" Brother Grifo's riddle arose yet again unbidden in my mind. But I told myself I had other things to think about and I began to plan in my mind's eye what I could create at Shaftesbury, unhindered by strange ideas such as those of Morcant.

I had become expert at carving flying angels or cherubim, in fact they were something of a speciality of mine. If the king was suggesting a carved decoration on the wall behind the altar I might carve a crucifix – a 'rood' we Anglo Saxons call it – and surmount it with a pair of them. Morcant's words flashed into my mind for a moment, "*Take it up*, not bow down to it ..." and the anticipatory pleasure dimmed a little but I pushed the remark aside.

The fyrdman who accompanied me was no talker and I was so absorbed in my plans and schemes that I did not notice the change in the weather at first. The light breeze dropped and the sky, which had been blue as a cornflower, began to cloud over. Then there was a sudden shower which definitely interrupted my reverie but which was over almost before it had begun. But when the huge drops mingled with hailstones had died away, the sky did not clear again and the wind began to rise. I looked at the fyrdman anxiously but he seemed impervious to the weather, humped silent and enduring on the horse's back more like a bale of pack goods than a man. We pressed on for a while until the wind suddenly dropped again, there was a clap of thunder and a tremendous storm of rain burst on us. Struggling to control my frightened mount I shouted to the fyrdman who at last seemed awake.

"There's a nun lives hereabouts," he shouted back. "I remember the spot. I'm sure she could shelter us until this is over – come on," and he turned his horse off the road down a rutted wagon track towards some farm buildings barely visible through the torrent.

The door of the imposing house was shut against the storm but we knocked and called and a man appeared from one of the outbuildings.

"Can you shelter travellers until the storm is over?" I shouted.

"Aye, quick, over here!" he called and we urged our poor horses gratefully towards him.

The building turned out to be a stable, adequate for several horses. With a "come in and welcome," the door was pulled open, then fastened behind us.

A great calm seemed to engulf us. The fury of the wind still roared outside but the air inside the stable was stiller and warm and smelled of sweet straw and hay. An old horse, quietly tugging fodder from a manger, regarded us curiously. The man who had welcomed us turned to greet us. In the dim light, which made its way into the stable only through cracks and crannies under the thatch and in the wattle walls, I thought I caught sight of a thrall collar – the iron neck ring which identified a slave.

"Where are you from and what is your errand, sirs?" he asked, and his softly modulated, almost singing, accent reminded me of Morcant's.

"We are from Leofham Burgh and are on our way to Shaftesbury," I replied. "I have a commission from the king to make certain wood carvings in the Abbey chapel."

"My mistress, the Nun Oswynn, will be glad to shelter you. She is always ready to welcome travellers; she has a daughter at the Abbey in Shaftesbury, and will be glad to speed you on your way." He began to help us unsaddle the horses, sparing no trouble to help us and finding us fodder and clean litter for the animals.

"I've never met a solitary nun before – 'vowesses' you call them, don't you?" I said. "I've just come back from Francia and vowesses are somewhat frowned upon there. The Franks think that if a widow wishes to become a nun she should go into a nunnery rather than living according to her vows on her own lands."

"Wessex is behind the times in such matters," said our new friend. "There are still many solitary nuns dotted around the kingdom living on their own estates with their own servants." He paused, patting the old horse and piling more hay into its manger. "My name is Adam, I am clerk to the Nun Oswynn and in charge of her little chapel. I'll go over to the house now and tell her there are visitors. Be pleased to make your way over as soon as the rain eases off. What names shall I give?"

I explained who we were and he hurried off to the house to tell his mistress of our arrival and make preparations for us, despite the continuing torrent. I had been correct about the thrall collar.

The Nun Oswynn, a plump and cheerful woman, proved to

be a convivial host. It quickly became apparent that she was not a nun for any great religious reasons. Her late husband's family were keen to keep his lands in their circle and wanted her to marry another distant relative; the family could lose out otherwise. But Oswynn would have none of it and rather than marry someone she did not like, she took vows and became a nun. A nunnery did not appeal to her at all but as a vowess or individual nun, she could live on her own property and leave it in her will to whoever she pleased. Her house reminded me of Thane Pelhere's old hall in my childhood days. The smoke made its way out through a hole in the thatch and the dogs were stretched out warming themselves by the fire. When she found I was on my way to Shaftesbury she was delighted.

"Ah! My daughter Leofrun is a novice at the Abbey there! She is such a saintly child – not a bit like me – nothing would satisfy her but the king's great new Abbey. A magnificent place it is, they tell me. The king has spared no expense. Fine buildings – and more planned – and a rich interior. Now, it might be useful to me that you are going there as I have some good ripe cheeses to send to my daughter. Could you take them for me?"

"I will gladly take them," I said. "Has your daughter been at the Abbey long?"

"Nearly a year now," said the nun, "and I tried hard to persuade her not to go. 'You'll regret it when you've been there a while,' I told her, but she would not listen. 'You are all keen on religion now that you have your freedom,' I said, 'but wait till you have had nothing but religion night and day for a few months then you'll think differently about it.'"

"But if she changes her mind, she can return to you, can't she?" I asked, knowing the more relaxed attitude of things in Wessex compared with Francia.

"I'll not risk my neck trying to get her out again once she's

# The Riddling Nun

taken her vows," replied the nun. "No one can take a nun away from a nunnery such as Shaftesbury Abbey without the king's express permission – it's against the law! I told her absolutely straightly that if she changed her mind I could not – would not – help her if she gets fed up with droning out the liturgy endlessly."

"But you must do that yourself here, surely," I said, "and you are, presumably, not tired of it."

"Oh, Adam says all the liturgy and so on for me in the chapel," she explained, "I sing one office a day, vespers, and he does all the rest."

"The Benedictines," I began loftily, "sing seven offices a day; the first is matins at midnight ..."

"My daughter may think she'll enjoy that but it would certainly not do for me," she interrupted with a laugh. "I like my sleep! But you're welcome to join us for vespers if you wish. The whole household is present for that."

When, in response to her inquiries, I told her that I had been in Francia for some time, she was interested and plied me with questions. Unfortunately they were mostly about the ladies' gowns, jewellery and hair styles so I was not able to be of much help to her. She herself wore a nun's veil or headdress but her gown was as rich and elegant as that of the Lady Edith at Leofham Burgh herself.

We filed into the little chapel for vespers. The household consisted of about ten female servants, and a few men to do the rough work as well as Adam. These, together with some of the nearby villagers, made up the congregation. There was a crude wooden rood on the wall of the chapel – I could have done a much better job. The service was not long, and consisted mostly of chanting Psalms in Latin. The nun had a loud rasping voice which dominated all the others. Then, while she fidgeted, coughed and smoothed her gown, Adam carefully read the Psalms that had been sung, but in Anglo-Saxon now, following this with a reading from the gospel in Latin which he again translated afterwards. Plainly glad when all this was over, the nun led the way back to the house where the servants at once began to finish the preparations for nothing short of a feast.

I am fond of good food and was ravenous after our long ride so I was delighted to see the barley bread trenchers laden with roast fowl dressed with savoury beans, spiced egg and crumbling white cheese. It was easy to see how the Nun Oswynn had arrived at her well-rounded shape if this was her daily fare. Glancing at the fyrdman who was my guide I could see that his attention was on the ale being brought in rather than the food. I hoped he would be in a fit state to continue guiding me the next morning. A harp was produced from somewhere and passed round, though the Nun Oswynn sensibly avoided singing herself. "I stick to telling riddles," she explained as the harp passed her by. "We'll have some of those later on. I've no voice for singing, although my clerk does his best to teach me!"

"Tell me," I asked her, "would I be right in thinking that your clerk is a Celt? I have a Celtic friend in holy orders and I think I catch a hint of the same accent in your clerk's voice."

"Young Adam? Yes he is," she replied. "His father was clerk to my father – he was born a thrall. I have granted him his freedom in my will if he keeps the chapel in good repair and sings his way through the Psalter every month when I'm gone. He is a wise young man, though he has some strange ideas of his own."

"So does my own Celtic friend," I murmured. "'Rome is wrong, Jerusalem is wrong and Antioch is wrong. Only the Scots and the Celts are right,' that's what one scholar wrote about their attitude; it's a national characteristic!"

Nevertheless, when the harp was passed to me, I thought I

# The Riddling Nun

would sing a song that I had learned from Morcant when he first came to Leofham and which had enchanted all our villagers. It tells in Anglo-Saxon verse the story of the creation and fall of man and begins:

> *This is the song that tells*
> *How being came to be*
> *This is the lay that opens wide*
> *The book of history.*
>
> *All things that something are*
> *Of nothing did God make*
> *In six full days the deed was done*
> *Then he his rest did take.*

As I had half expected, Adam was riveted. When I had finished, he leaned over and asked, "Where did you learn that song, Master? My father used to sing it – or something quite like it – to me when I was tiny but he sang in our own tongue not Anglo-Saxon."

I was in the middle of telling him all about Morcant when the Nun Oswynn rapped on the table and announced, "Now then, a riddle: I am like the snow and yet not cold, I am like water yet none can see through me, I am food for man and beast yet none can eat me. Eve gave me but did not receive me. What am I?"

I flatter myself that I am quick with riddles and this was an easy one. Like snow must mean something white ... and like water ... a liquid then. A white liquid? Food, yes, but not eaten? Well, you can't eat a liquid you have to drink it. A white liquid drink – must be milk. As for the bit about Eve, she gave milk to her babies, of course, but was never a baby herself so ... "Milk?" I queried.

The Nun Oswynn laughed, delighted, "You have a quick wit for a riddle, Master Wulfgar," she said. "Have you one for us now?"

We Anglo-Saxons enjoy riddles and I had quite a store of them

# Wulfgar and the Riddle

in the back of my mind – but which ones would already be familiar to the nun? I cast my mind back.

"I carry a mighty giant in my hand. His cradle is a cup from which no man drinks. His brother, which sprang from the same noble parent, feeds the swine. What do I carry in my hand?"

This was far too easy for the nun. "An acorn, of course," she said at once. "I'm afraid I've heard that before. Now, here is a holy riddle for you. I got this one from someone who heard it from a monk: I died once yet am ever dying. When you cut me out of a great stone, I am worthy of worship and honour. When you dress me with gold and gems you carry me hither and yon to guard you from evil spirits. What am I?"

I was tongue tied and could not reply: not because I did not know the answer but because I thought I did.

# Chapter 6
# Shaftesbury

The answer to the nun's riddle – the Riddle of the Rood she said it was called – was, as I had guessed, the rood or crucifix. It was a riddle that would have filled Morcant with horror and I must admit I was also a little taken aback by what it took for granted. "I died once yet am ever dying." Christ died on the cross but if his body and blood are always really present at the Lord's Supper then he dies again and again. "When you cut me out of a great stone, I am worthy of worship and honour." That referred to the great stone crosses at market places and outside churches. "When you dress me with gold and gems you carry me hither and yon to guard you from evil spirits." This signified the small jewelled crosses and crucifixes wealthy people carried about as jewellery. What did Morcant call them, magic talismans? I went to bed with my mind unsettled again.

When the huge basket of hard round cheeses and I made our way up the hill to the gate of Shaftesbury Abbey the next day, it was a little past noon. The fyrdman and his headache had gone off to find the detachment of the fyrd which he was detailed to join. This, apparently, was in another quarter of the town. I can't say I was sorry to lose him for it had not been a pleasant journey although he and his pain in the head were only a part of the problem. The rain-washed meadows had been dotted with new lambs, snowy white beside their tawny dams. Tiny violets, pale primroses, starry stitchwort and nodding windflowers had jewelled the hedgerows with brittle colours and the sharp scent of

## Wulfgar and the Riddle

wild garlic had mingled with the bittersweet smell of new-turned fallow. All this teeming life would normally have delighted me but my heart had been heavy and my mind gave me no rest. The incessant joy of the throstle, "Cul-dee, Cul-dee, did-he-do-it? Did-he-do-it?" far from raising my spirits, was irritating.

I had not slept well at the nun's house. The face of the robber, though it still haunted me whenever I shut my eyes, was beginning to fade a little. Although he was waiting in the back of my mind until my other cares and concerns were clouded with drowsiness, if I opened my eyes he vanished. But then Brother Grifo's riddle came back to me yet again and my mind could get no rest.

As we rode through the gentle April countryside I had continued to turn the nun's Riddle of the Rood over and over in my mind, like one who did not know the solution. Yet I did know and it disturbed me. My reflections, as the fyrdman rode silently beside me, did not improve my temper. I had felt angry with Morcant. Why ever should he bother his head with all this! Other people just got on with things without questioning and delving into everything. Just because he insisted on only the Scripture for guidance! No wonder the king kept him firmly out of the way in Leofham. Such ideas were dangerously near heresy, whatever Mariwig might say about, "never been condemned by any authority of the church." And why tell *me* all about it? What was I, a wood carver of all things, supposed to do about it? And meddlers like Ratramnus and Claudius of Turin – I had felt angry with them too. Worst of all, I had found, try as I might, that I could not wholly convince my own mind that they were wrong. And that had left me without a basis for my new-found self-confidence and without a basis for much of the work that earned my daily bread ...

It was only now, with the fyrdman gone about his business, when I was right outside the gates of the Abbey and the porter was pushing open his little window-shutter to ask me who I was and what I wanted that I knew what I ought to do.

I would pray. Every day I would go down on my knees and cry out, "Help me, O Lord, to know thy truth in this question!" until this whole riddle sorted itself out – at least in my own head – and I knew what on earth to do about it.

A sense of relief swept over me and I answered the porter's gruff enquiry with a smile, "Wulfgar Waelwulfson, wood carver, lately of Corvey Abbey in Francia, at your service. I am on a commission from the king to do carved work in the Abbey chapel and from the Nun Oswynn to deliver twelve ripe cheese to her daughter, the Novice Leofrun!"

# Chapter 7
# Æthelgifu and Eadwulfu

Never having met an abbess before, I was confused. Of the two ladies in front of me, which was the Abbess Æthelgifu to whom I should present the letter from the king? Tall and stately, the standing figure was the obvious candidate. Not a wisp of hair strayed from under her tight wimple and veil. Her belted habit was of a coarse grey wool exactly appropriate for an abbess and a bunch of keys and an ivory crucifix on a chain hung at her waist. There was a grim set to her thin-lipped mouth and there were deep downward-pointing lines at its corners. The sharpness of her small black eyes, set in a reddish countenance, also marked her out as someone in a position of authority. The other much younger lady, hardly more than a girl, was seated. Her dress was almost identical to that of the standing figure but her appearance could not have been more different. Her slight frame was thin and wasted and her face was pale. The eyes, however, were frank, kind and yet strangely penetrating. Where had I seen such eyes before? Of course! How could I forget, even for a moment? I stepped forward and knelt before the seated Abbess Æthelgifu and presented to her as I did so the letter from her father, whose generous but piercing eyes seemed to look out at me from her face. "Good Lady Abbess," I said, "I have here a letter from your royal father who has asked me to come in respect of some carvings for the new chapel."

To my astonishment the standing figure lent over without a word and took the letter from my hands, broke open the seal and began to scan the contents! Had I been mistaken? Surely not!

"But you must be Wulfgar!" said the pale, seated lady. "My father has told me much about you and your work. I am so glad you have come. What does my father write, Eadwulfu?"

The grim mouth snapped open, "The king hopes you are in better health, Abbess, and sends this young man," she looked down her nose at me, "to carve whatever fittings you desire for the abbey chapel. I must say," she added, screwing up her little piggy eyes as she looked at me, "he seems young. I was expecting someone with more experience."

"But you are experienced, are you not, Master Wulfgar?" asked the young abbess, gesturing for me to stand up. "My father said you had just returned from the great Abbey of Corvey in Francia – and also that he has seen a dragon's head carved by you that is so life-like that he thought for a moment it was real!"

"I am honoured by my king's compliments, Lady Abbess," I said, "but such skill as I have comes from God, it is not of my doing."

The Nun Eadwulfu made a slight snorting noise. "No doubt you have brought some sample of your work," she said.

I began to dislike this woman. "I'm afraid not," I said, "but I have brought twelve ripe cheeses for the Novice Leofrun from her mother the Nun Oswynn!" and I lugged the huge basket into view from the doorway where I had left it.

"Cheeses!" The Nun Eadwulfu was suddenly more enthusiastic. "I will have the sacristan called to take charge of them at once."

"But, Eadwulfu, they were sent for the Novice Leofrun," said the Abbess gently. "She must at least see them! Have her called and she can make sure they go down to the stores herself."

Lodgings had been found for me in a house in the town belonging to an old widow called Wynflæd which was built

## Æthelgifu and Eadwulfu

against the abbey wall. The place was clean and comfortable, if not very private, but old Wynflæd was an endless talker and I wondered if I would ever get any peace. I think she had given me a complete description of every nun in the Abbey before I had been there half an hour! She plainly had an intimate knowledge of the royal foundation, under whose walls her little house sheltered, and *all* its inmates. For the Abbess Æthelgifu she had the greatest respect and devotion: for the Nun Eadwulfu she had none.

"The king's daughter is a dear lady," she rattled on, "and so poorly in her health. Sometimes she can't even stand. But she is in the chapel at every office even so – why, they *carry* her in sometimes! Not fit to do any work herself beyond praying, she isn't – that's why that rogue of a woman Eadwulfu runs the place! Oh, you haven't seen it but you will," she responded to my half-hearted attempt to protest, "with a rod of iron too! And greedy with it – don't I know it? I help in the cooking sometimes when they're busy and she eats more than the rest of them put together. Shocking it is! I don't know where she puts it all – she's like a bean pole! You'll steer clear of her, Master Wood-Carver, if you take my advice, and get your orders direct from the dear Abbess herself."

Among many other things I learned that the Abbess Æthelgifu, out of concern for the tired nuns who had to stand through the offices and vigils as well as working all day, had ordered benches (a thing I had never heard of in any church or chapel in all my travels) to be put in the chapel. Eadwulfu would have objected, said Wynflæd, if she had not been glad to be able to sit down herself. Wynflæd was also indignant that, despite not producing a single stitch herself, Eadwulfu drove the nuns harshly to produce endless quantities of ecclesiastical embroidery, forcing them to unpick the slightest unevenness in their stitchery and making no allowances for those with poor sight or less ability in the craft. The only thing that ever freed the nuns from the scourge of her attention was winter weather. The room in which they had to work was freezing, the windows being open in order for the nuns

# Wulfgar and the Riddle

to see, and no fire was allowed lest the smoke should taint the work. Eadwulfu preferred to take herself off somewhere warmer.

When I mentioned the Novice Leofrun, Wynflæd was interested. "Really! So you know her mother!" she said. "Now there's a girl that's changed – and I put it down to that horrible Eadwulfu! – No hear me out – Leofrun, she came here all full of life and bright-like – I'm not saying she was flighty like some of them, mind – just cheerful more, you'd say. And now look at her! Whatever she was looking for in an Abbey, she found it was different from what she expected, I think. Not that she'd shirk hard work that one, oh no. She's busy in the dairy and with the fowls every day and I know she's good with her needle but there's some girls who think they can come to a place like this and all be heavenly minded together. Well, it does not work! A saint would have a hard struggle with all that goes on in this place, I can tell you. Well, you look at her face now and you can see it. No joy there now to be sure. Properly glum whenever you see her."

I remembered the Nun Oswynn's warning to her daughter. "I suppose she has grown tired of so much strict religious observance," I said.

Wynflæd shook her head. "I don't think so, not that one. She's more likely to think there's not enough of it. No, she's the saintly type and it's my guess she's found out that most of them in there are not."

It was plain that there would be no peaceful corner in Wynflæd's tiny house for me to pray at all, let alone to pray as I had decided about the riddle that was perplexing me. But I was determined not to give up the idea before I had even begun it, so after a bowl of excellent pottage supplied by Wynflæd I took myself off outside to look for a suitable spot.

The stone walls of the Abbey seemed massive, towering up into the evening air and I wondered if they too had be made of

# Æthelgifu and Eadwulfu

the stones of the old "giants". For a short stretch the little houses, like that of Wynflæd, continued up against the wall making a little street alongside it. Their doors stood open and the sounds of family mealtimes wafted out – pots and spoons and lively chatter. Then the houses seemed to peter out. There was a stable, some sort of shed, a space where some unused building materials were stacked, some kale plots and then a grassy area on which a tethered horse was grazing. Here, right by the edge of the walls, stood an old apple tree.

The builders had taken care not to destroy the tree. It had evidently not suffered from disturbance during the building of the Abbey wall for it was strong and healthy and smothered in fragile blossom. A blackbird had stationed himself on the topmost branch and, carefully considered, phrase by phrase, his music floated out over the still evening air. Above the walls I could just catch a glimpse of what I guessed was part of the chapel roof. As I lingered on the petal-strewn grass under the tree listening to the blackbird, I became aware of sounds on the other side of the wall, footsteps approaching, all crunching and hurrying together along a gravelled path, but no voices. Of course! The nuns would be making their way to the chapel for vespers. No doubt Eadwulfu did not allow any talking en route!

The footsteps died away and I wondered if I could worm my way into the recess behind the old tree. That would be an out of the way spot, certainly. In fact, it was an ideal place; even the blackbird did not notice me but went on singing and listening, singing and listening as I squeezed into the dry nook behind his tree. One low broken branch actually lent against the wall, and I knelt down to pray, resting my arms and head on its mossy surface. Before I could begin my prayer, however, another sound floated over the Abbey walls and mingled with the blackbird's song. It was so beautiful that it took my breath away and for a moment I could not imagine what it was. A searingly sweet melody seemed to climb and climb and then float down like the petals of the apple blossom

71

in a clear, undulating wave of unbroken beauty, refreshing as soft spring rain. Was heaven opening so that I could hear the song of the angels? I looked up but there was nothing above me but apple blossom, the wall of the Abbey and the roof of the chapel. The chapel! Of course! I was hearing the nuns' vespers! I listened, wondering at the contrast between Wynflæd's descriptions of the frictions of Abbey life and the graceful and faultless unison of this psalmody. Not until the evening psalms died to a close did I lay my head on the mossy branch and pray as I had intended in simple words such as I had always used in prayer before I went away to Francia, "Help me, Dear Lord, to know the truth. I am perplexed but I would follow my Saviour. Help me and bend my will to yours in all things."

Despite the comfort of my new lodgings it was still difficult to get to sleep at first. The robber's wild face started to loom over me but I managed to shut it out. Then the riddle and my discussions with Morcant bothered me. But I had prayed for guidance and I trusted that I would get it. At length old Wynflæd's steady snores began to rise up in the darkness, so incongruous both with the image of the robber and my other thoughts that sleep stole over me, deep and dreamless.

# Chapter 8
# Embroidery

As I worked away at the tasks I had been given in the chapel over the next few days, I became starkly aware that Wynflæd's waspish remarks gave an only too accurate picture of Abbey life. There was little of celestial consonance here; only dark discord. The exception was the Abbess Æthelgifu. Around her spread concord and harmony and wherever she was the atmosphere was melodious.

She had begun by taking me round the chapel and explaining her ideas. She was strong that day and free of pain. She walked up and down the new building with me, pointing out the things she thought I might do. I told her that I had heard the nuns at vespers the previous day and shyly mentioned the beauty of the singing. She smiled.

"Yes, it is heavenly," she said, "but it takes much painstaking practice. It is so hard for the novices to learn. Eadwulfu is a good teacher, of course. But even she gets impatient sometimes. They have to hear things over and over before they can remember them correctly and it is exhausting work which takes hours of instruction and reduces them to tears, time after time."

By the time we had finished our walk around there was a quantity of work laid out for me, yet she had not mentioned a rood.

"What would you like me to put on that wall over there?" I asked, pointing to the obvious place. I had been hesitating to bring the matter up. If she did not want such a thing, in my present state of mind, perhaps it would be easier if I did not have to make one.

The abbess sighed. "I know what my father would have there, and why he has sent you," was her surprising answer, "but I have my doubts. Have you not seen, Carver Wulfgar, how the poor people worship the rood? I am sure that is not what I read of in the Holy Scriptures – but you are a wood carver. I cannot think that you would agree with me."

I looked at her in astonishment. "Lady Abbess," I replied, "I think ... that is, I have heard ... I have been praying for light on this very subject and I ... "

She seemed relieved and smiled at me as she interrupted, "Then we will leave that wall for the present at least," she said.

I looked at the benches. Crude they were, just planks on logs. In my mind's eye I could see just what a different and tasteful job *I* would have made of such chapel furnishings. I would have taken the opportunity to create something rich and worthy and I would have been able to do it superbly. Whoever had made these paltry things had probably done his best but quite frankly they were primitive. Now if I had been given the task ...

I was about to put all this into suitable words for the Lady Abbess's hearing when suddenly, for the first time, it struck me that this was a conceited and rather unpleasant way of looking at my own work. So I bit my tongue and said merely: "I have never seen benches in a chapel before; would you like me to decorate them a little?"

"Could you?" She seemed surprised. "Well, yes, if you can. I know it *is* unusual but the poor dears are so tired sometimes; they just need to sit down. Eadwulfu says I am too lenient with them. Her methods are strict. She says that if they are made to suffer here below then they will face less punishment in the next life. This is the basis of her system of discipline but I do not find any mention in God's Word of any punishment for Christians after death. She means well. She is devoted to the cross and worships devoutly before the relics of the Saint and the fragment of the true cross which we have in a casket here in the Abbey. She is often on her knees for hours and yet ... I am sometimes afraid that what she is doing might be all wrong ... so much pain and ... and harshness ... "

"I'll see what I can do with the benches," I said, feeling that it was not my place to comment on such remarks, however much I might begin to sympathise with them.

Æthelgifu left me to make my measurements and sketch out what was needed for some panels she had asked for. I knew these would require good seasoned wood and it might be a while before I could find anyone in Shaftesbury who thought they could supply me. Then it would probably have to be fetched from somewhere or other and the time would drag on. At least I could set to work on the benches in the meantime. The baulks of timber from which they were crudely thrown together were thick enough for me to turn the ends into animal shapes, perhaps a different animal for each bench. I was just examining the legs to see if I could make them look like the relevant animal's feet when rapid footsteps came marching through the chapel. I looked up. Eadwulfu was standing in front of me.

"Ah, here you are," she said. "I've a job for you. Come this way," and without so much as a please or thank you, she turned, beckoning me to follow her out of the chapel.

I picked up my new tool bag and Eadwulfu led the way back into the Abbey itself. She took me to a large airy room with open windows all down one side in which some ten or so nuns were busy embroidering. At a lectern stood another nun who paused in her reading as we entered.

"You can carry on in a moment, Æbbe," said Eadwulfu to the reader. "I just have to show the wood carver what is needed," and she marched me over to one of the windows where a shutter was dangling loose.

"It needs mending," she said. "You can do a simple job like that I'm sure. Æbbe, you may continue to read."

"... now there was in the monastery of this Abbess Hild a certain brother, marked out specially by God's grace. He was accustomed to compose religious and holy songs ..." The Nun Æbbe was not a good reader. Her dreary voice intoned from the book as I grumpily examined the broken window shutter. This was not the work the king had sent me to do and Eadwulfu had not even asked if I would mind! ("... and he could turn anything taught to him out of the Holy Scriptures into sweet and penitential verses in his native language ...") But there was nothing here I could not fix. I opened my tool bag. ("... he was well advanced in years yet he had never learned anything of poetry and so sometimes at a banquet, if he saw the harp come towards him, he would rise up from table ...")

Eadwulfu was pacing round the room slowly inspecting all the work. I began dismantling the shutter. ("... having left the banquet he went to the stable, for he had to look after the cattle that night, and went to sleep. Suddenly someone was standing by him in his sleep, and greeting him by name ...") I noticed two of the nuns were working at a large embroidery frame. Eadwulfu stopped to inspect their work. ("... But he replied, 'I cannot sing, that is why I left the banquet and came here, because I could not sing.' Then the one who talked to him said, 'Nevertheless, you must sing to me.' 'What must I sing?' he asked. 'Sing the beginning of creation ...'")

"One moment, Æbbe," Eadwulfu's voice cut across the tale from Bede's *History*, "you will unpick that disgraceful piece of work, Berta, and take care that you do not damage the fabric as you do so. Our stitches will be *even* and *neat*, those you have made could be bettered by a three year old. I have had reason to tell you of this before. Continue, Æbbe."

# Embroidery

"... 'Sing the beginning of creation,' said the stranger. So at once he began to sing verses praising the God of Creation. He had never heard this song before and it went like this: 'Now must we praise the Creator of the kingdom of heaven, the Creator's omnipotence ... '"

I looked across at poor Berta after this rebuke. I judged her to be quite an old woman and as she struggled with her task I wondered how well she could see. She was weeping silently and I felt sorry for her. The young nun who was working with her, glanced at Eadwulfu to see that her back was turned and then, slipping her own needle securely into the fabric, she motioned Berta to stop and began swiftly unpicking the faulty stitches. Æbbe's flat and unmusical voice droned on. "... So when he woke up, he remembered all that he had sung in his dream, and even added more in the same style, beautiful words which expressed God's praise well ... "

I had the shutter down now, laid on the floor. I glanced up out of the window. ("In the morning he went to the reeve ... ") I noticed Wynflæd leaving the Abbey dairy, ("... he was taken to the abbess ... ") she was wiping her hands on her apron and walking swiftly towards the gates. ("... they all considered that grace had been given to him from heaven itself ... ") I started to dismantle the base of the shutter.

"... The abbess, saw with joy God's grace in the man ... " Eadwulfu held up her hand. "One moment, Æbbe. I regret, dear sisters, that I have to leave you for a short time. You will continue your work as best you can without my assistance. Continue, Æbbe," and with that she walked briskly out of the door without even waiting to hear Æbbe's monotone reading recommence.

For a moment or two everything did continue – exactly as she had left it. Æbbe droned on and the other nuns stitched quietly. But, as soon as they judged Eadwulfu well out of earshot, a kind of muted pandemonium broke out. Æbbe's voice died away and everyone was whispering at once: "She's gone to help herself to some cream and new cheese now the coast is clear, the old cat."

# Wulfgar and the Riddle

"Yes, I saw old Wynflæd leave the dairy for the day."

"Who knows a good riddle – quick! Anything's better than that old stuff you're reading, Æbbe!"

"If only I could sit by the window," – this was Berta – "I could see what I'm doing."

"What a gown I could make for myself with this stuff! And it has to be a cope for a bishop! What a waste!"

"Here Æbbe! You've got a good figure – drape it round you, there! What does that look like?"

The simpering Æbbe, her reading abandoned, obligingly paraded round the room with the half-finished cope draped over her shoulders making comic gestures that had the others in suppressed hoots of laughter. Only one nun remained silent, the young one who had unpicked Berta's bad stitches. She was sewing away for dear life and not at her own work but at Berta's.

"Come on, Leofrun," said someone suddenly. "You have a go. That silk and those shimmering colours would just suit you!" but the young nun only shook her head silently and pressed on stitching at Berta's embroidery.

"Eadwulfu's pet!"

"Nun Ne'er-do-Wrong!"

"Leave her alone, please dears," whispered Berta, hoarsely. "You know she's no favourite of Eadwulfu's and can't you see she's only trying to help me?"

The voices grew louder now that they were sure Eadwulfu was well out of earshot, "What about a riddle then?"

"Go on, tell us one, Leofrun!"

## Embroidery

"No, you'll get nothing like that out of Nun Goody-Goody!"

"Why not ask the young carpenter?" said someone suddenly. "He's bound to know some *very* funny ones!"

I felt hot with embarrassment. The last thing I wanted was to get involved in all this mischief. I was saved from the difficulty, however. Æbbe was still parading round the room in the embroidered cope and a nun at the back stuck her foot out as she passed. Æbbe came down with a crash and a rending sound. The room went absolutely silent.

# Chapter 9
# Leofrun

A babble of frightened voices broke out, "Now look what you've done!"

"You'll be in trouble! She'll fry you alive!"

"Can we fix it?"

"How badly is it torn?"

"Let me see!"

"Are you hurt, Æbbe?"

"Mind how you get up or you'll make the tear worse."

Only Leofrun and old Berta seemed to keep their heads. Quickly, they picked up the cope and inspected the damage. Arranging it carefully on the table where a little nun with a spotty face had originally been working on it, Leofrun began tacking the rent together. "Look, it's not too bad," she said, "it's only down the line of this gold thread-work here. Do you think you can manage to re-do it and take in the repair at the same time? See, you can just give this lion an extra long tail here and a bit more stem to these acanthus leaves and it will hardly notice!" The little nun was shaking but she took up her needle and worked with a will, following the line of Leofun's tacks with swift and neat stitches.

"I've no more gold thread left," she whispered – everyone was silent now holding their breath – "look, it's running out."

"I know where she keeps it," said Berta. "Shall I just take another reel?"

Leofrun hesitated. I guessed that all the gold thread was carefully weighed and accounted for since it was so valuable.

"No, I'll get it," she said.

Swiftly she opened a big chest full of bobbins and selected what she needed, breaking off a short length and replacing the reel.

Not much had been done to the window shutter while all this was going on. I could see that, if I did not have something to show her, I would also be implicated in any trouble that Eadwulfu detected when she returned. I glanced out of the window as I turned to get on with my work and saw with horror that Eadwulfu was emerging from the dairy. She stooped under the low doorway and then strode purposefully towards the Abbey house. Almost before I thought what I was doing, I had called out, "Quick, she's coming back!"

There was a panic. Æbbe rushed to the reading desk. I noticed she had the sense to turn over a couple of pages before starting to read. Leofrun delivered the length of spun gold to the trembling little nun and helped her thread her needle. "Just keep working normally," she said quietly. "She will probably never notice – and you, Carpenter! Stop gawping at us and get on with something!"

Somewhat stung by this rudeness, I pulled out some nails and began hammering the broken parts of the bottom of the shutter together again, almost drowning out Bede's *History* completely as I did so. Leofrun began to make her way back to her place beside Berta but Eadwulfu must have put on a burst of speed. The door opened, Eadwulfu entered and Leofrun was still in the centre of the room.

I stopped hammering and Æbbe's voice died away. Eadwulfu looked round the silent room taking in everything. Her normally florid red face was almost completely white except for one red spot on her cheek that seemed to throb with colour. She said absolutely nothing and Leofrun continued walking steadily back to her place.

Eadwulfu watched her with exaggerated deliberateness. Then she said, "I see you have finished your work, Novice Leofrun. I must see it. No doubt it is up to your usual high standard," and she strode across to the frame where Berta and Leofrun had been working. "Well, well, well, not a stitch done since I left! How do you account for it, Novice Leofrun? What have you been doing when you should have been sewing?"

Leofrun said nothing. She looked straight at the angry woman in silence. For a moment no one spoke and then Berta said, "She's been helping me."

Eadwulfu looked at the frame closely for a moment then she said, "Ah, yes. So I see. Very neat work, Novice Leofrun, very neat indeed. And that explains why she was standing in the middle of the room does it? Novice Leofrun, you will go to the scriptorium."

Leofrun walked calmly towards the door.

"Wait there until I can deal with you," stabbed Eadwulfu. She signalled to Æbbe and the monotone started up again. I shuddered, thinking how little I would like to be "dealt with" by Eadwulfu.

I had just finished the repair to the window when the door opened again. This time it was the gentle face of the Abbess Æthelgifu that appeared, wreathed in smiles. "I was looking for the wood carver," she explained. "Ah! there he is! O, Eadwulfu, my dear, you look most unwell! Do go and rest – there is still some time before Sext," and she stood aside, a slender figure hardly more than a girl, holding open the door and motioning Eadwulfu through it.

For a moment I thought Eadwulfu would refuse to go. She opened her mouth – and then seemed to change her mind and with a reverent bow of the head towards Æthelgifu she swept out of the room.

The whole room seemed to relax. The young abbess told Æbbe to rest her voice for a while and walked round all the embroidery frames making pleasant and encouraging remarks before arriving at the window where I was now packing up my tools.

"Thank you so much!" she exclaimed when she saw what I had done. "Did Eadwulfu ask you to do it? What a good idea! I do hope you didn't mind." As a matter of fact I *had* minded at the time but that seemed irrelevant now and I felt I could do any job, large or small, for the kind and gentle Abbess. A thought struck me and I said, "Now that the window is properly fixed, Lady Abbess, would it be possible to move those nuns with weaker eyes nearer to the light?" Of course, there was no connection whatever between fixing the shutter and moving the weak-eyed nuns near the window but it gave me an excuse to mention it.

Æthelgifu looked at me shrewdly with those penetrating blue eyes. "What an excellent idea!" she said, adding, "There is a cupboard door off its hinges and a broken shelf in the scriptorium, you know, but I hardly like to ask you to ... I mean you are a carver not a carpenter but I came to find you in case you would not mind ... "

"Oh, I'd be happy to help," I said at once, "I'll go there now, shall I?"

# Chapter 10
# The Scriptorium

The scriptorium was also the Abbey library. The books were housed in low closed book cases with reading desks on top and when I entered, Leofrun was engrossed in reading one of the huge volumes.

"I hope I'm not intruding, Nun Leofrun," I began, "but I've been asked to mend some bookcases."

Her eyes opened wide.

"Not by Nun Eadwulfu," I explained. "By the Abbess herself."

"I see," she said with a little laugh. "That explains it."

I set to work locating the broken cupboard. I thought back to what I had heard about this novice from her mother and from Wynflæd. If I was going to find out the truth about whether she was disappointed with life at Shaftesbury, if I was maybe going to try to help her, I did not have long; Eadwulfu would surely be here at any minute. There was no time to ease into the subject so I blurted out bluntly, "Are you happy here?"

"Why do you ask?" she said, greatly surprised.

I found the broken cupboard and got out my tools. "Because I have met your mother, the Nun Oswynn, and because I lodge with that old chatterbox, Wynflæd, who says you are not."

"You know my mother!" she was even more surprised.

"Listen, Leofrun, there is not much time. Eadwulfu will be here any moment. If you are not happy I might be able to help."

To my distress her eyes filled with tears. "Wynflæd is a good soul but she talks too much," she said. "You are kind, and I think I could trust you, but as to helping me I'm afraid no one can do that."

"Don't cry," I said, feeling rather useless. "Look, you are still only a novice; surely you can get out of the Abbey altogether if you wish. I know your mother says she could not – and would not – get you out if you changed your mind once you've taken your vows but now ... "

"I'm longing to go!" she said, with a kind of shuddering sob, "but when I try to explain to the Lady Abbess she is so sweet. She tells me to be patient and bear it for a little longer and who could refuse her?"

I could easily imagine the persuasiveness of such an encounter. "But in the end," I said, "she will surely let you go."

I could see her taking herself in hand and the tears subsided. "Yes, but she is so often ill," she explained, "and I'm so afraid of Eadwulfu! If the Abbess is ill – really ill – so that she can't come to the chapel, Eadwulfu will find a way to ... to force me through the vows. She has threatened to do it and she is a totally ruthless woman. Novices do *not* leave Shaftesbury – they know too much about who is really in charge ... "

This was more serious than I had imagined but before I could think of anything – offer some sort of help – she was speaking again. "I don't want you to think I'm just tired of religious observances; I know that's what my mother thought would happen. I'm not even tired of the bullying, the silliness, the pettiness, the constant

# The Scriptorium

grinding work; though it's bad enough as you have seen. No, it's far worse than that."

She paused and drew a deep breath. "There's nothing in it, Master Wood Carver. It's empty. It's just a rigmarole gone through. I came because I thought I would find God here; that I would be able to know him. I *knew* there would be other nuns who were here for no good reason, I *knew* it would be hard work but I was sure – so sure – that if I became a nun, God would be pleased with me. If I were able to kiss the holy box in which the bones of the saint are lying, if I went through the daily office, over and over, over and over, the blessed words would somehow bring me closer to him until I was truly holy myself. But it's like a riddle with no answer for I'm no holier than before – no different. No, that's not true – I am different. Now I wonder if there is *any God at all*; I never, ever thought like that before. All this religion seems like so much rubbish now; maybe the very idea of God is rubbish too! Oh dear, you must be shocked."

Here was something at least that I could try to help with. "Not so shocked as you might think," I replied as I re-fixed the cupboard door where it belonged. "I once had a dear friend who doubted that God existed but God was good to him and sent a messenger of the truth to him – and to me also."

She did not answer so I continued, "I am not surprised that you cannot find your own way to God. Pray to him to find you!"

"Do you think I do not pray?" she exclaimed, "I spend hours! *Pater Noster, qui es in caelis, sanctificetur nomen tuum ...*"

"Do you never go down on your knees and say, 'Lord, I'm lost. I don't know the way. Please find me'?"

She looked astounded.

"What were you reading?" I asked. The book was still open on the desk, the golden headed ivory aestel, or reader's pointer, lying by the page.

*The Life of Saint Cuthbert*, she said, picking up the aestel carefully as she spoke, "and I'm not sure I believe a word of it. Miracles, power over animals and birds, silly stories about a body that will not rot away after death. That's for the credulous. I don't think anyone here believes it really either, although they would all say they did. I'm not surprised people in monasteries made this sort of stuff up. If they were like the nuns here, they probably did it for a bit of fun to see what they could get away with!"

"I see," I said, "You think the book is untrustworthy – it probably is – do not search for the truth in it, then. You understand Latin well enough, you would not be your father's daughter if you did not, so go to God's Word itself and read that. Pray to God for his Holy Spirit to open your eyes as you read and he will do it – I know this from personal experience."

Her eyes opened wide. "Pray just like that, in my own tongue?" she asked. "I suppose I never thought God understood any language but Latin – but of course that's a silly idea!"

I had started work on the rickety shelf now, hammering in nails and smoothing down a rough corner. Suddenly, for the first time since I returned home to Wessex, I felt as if I really *had* come back to something. Whatever it was I had learned in Francia it was not useful to me now. I found myself wanting to talk to Leofrun just the way Morcant would have talked to her. Nothing I had gleaned from the learned monks of Corvey would be of the slightest help to this poor girl. She needed God's plain simple word and there was only one place to find it. The knotty riddle began to dissolve before my eyes.

She stood watching me as I worked until the shelf was ready to go back into place. Then she said, "From personal experience? I

The Scriptorium

have never met anyone who witnessed miracles like those in that book." She pointed at *The Life of Saint Cuthbert*, "Yet what you are telling me would be a kind of miracle, wouldn't it?"

"Yes," I said, "Jesus once told his disciples that they would do greater miracles than he did. He did *not* mean those things you are reading about in that book. He was talking about the miracle that would happen when people, hundreds of them – thousands of them, believed their preaching – the miracle of the new birth ..." I could see she could not understand what I was talking about. There was so little time! Eadwulfu could walk in at the door at any minute. If Leofrun read the books of Scripture for herself, I was sure the difference between the miracles of Scripture and mere old wives' tales would become clear to her. "Look," I said, "where is there a copy of the books of Holy Scripture in this library?" She took me to a desk where a huge volume lay open surrounded by all the pens, penknives, ink and smooth wax writing tablets for making notes that make up the scribe's equipment.

"Here is part of it," she said.

I glanced at the open volume. It was a copy of Matthew's Gospel. The text was in the centre of the pages in large letters and round it was an ocean of smaller letters – some gloss extracted and boiled down from the works of the Church Fathers. The book was incomplete and on the opened pages before us now the gloss petered out leaving only the large centre column. Evidently the second stage of copying the gloss was in progress and the initial copying of the main text had been completed. "Fetch the aestel here and read this," I said, "with all your might and main, read it. Not the glosses in the margin – don't waste your time with those – just the actual Scripture, the big letters in the middle of the page. Pray for the guidance of the Holy Spirit to know the truth and I will pray for you also." I glanced up through the window. "I'd better move," I said, gathering up my tools as I

89

spoke. "Here comes Eadwulfu, but you are in luck! The Abbess herself is with her! Look, I'm going to try to help, but for now promise me, you will read the book just as I've said."

She nodded solemnly, as though sealing a pact between us, and turned to fetch the glittering aestel as I slipped out of the door.

# Chapter 11
# The Go-Between

For days I saw no more of Leofrun but she was constantly in my thoughts. I evolved plan after plan to get her safely back to her mother but discarded every one as impractical in some way or other. I worked at my task with the benches in the chapel, slipping outside to sit in the pale sunshine when I knew the nuns would be coming to sing their way through the psalter. I could not get Leofrun out of my mind. In the evenings when I wormed my way into the little space behind the old apple tree, it was for her I prayed far more than for myself. Another curious thing happened too. Just once or twice instead of the cruel haunting face of the wild robber appearing when I closed my eyes at night, it was Leofrun's little white face I saw. My uneasy mind at once relaxed and, before I could wonder about it, I was asleep.

I located someone in Shaftesbury who would be able to sort out some of the timber I needed; it seemed it would take a frustratingly long time. The Abbess had not seemed to want a rood so perhaps she would also be less than keen on the angels I had had in mind. Then one morning I had the chance to discuss it with her again.

I was working my way steadily through the benches. I had the idea of putting a domestic animal on one end and a wild animal on the other end of each bench. On the first, for example, I had a sheep at one end with curling wool and magnificent horns. At the other end was a wolf, his tongue lolling out of his mouth. Each end had feet to match too, the sheep with her cloven hoof, the wolf

## Wulfgar and the Riddle

with his doggy paw and strong claws. Another bench I decorated with a horse at one end and a deer at the other and so on through a gamut of animals. My latest creature was a cow. I decided I would balance it at the opposite end with a wild boar for its companion. I was working away at the details one morning, giving the cow some grass and flowers dripping out of her mouth, when the Abbess herself walked in.

"I just had to come and tell you," she began, "how delighted we all are with these animals. They are enchanting; they make me think of all creation praising the creator. And do you know," she laughed, "the nuns find your wolf so realistic they are rather shy of sitting next to him!"

I was glad at this for I had never seen a real live wolf and my carving included some guesswork.

"I had wondered about some flying angels," I said timidly, "on the wall ..."

"I know, I know ..." she said, almost as if she could read my thoughts, "but you see ..." it was she who was hesitating now, "I don't know what you'd think about this but I'm not keen on anything that would give the wrong impression. I mean, it might make the nuns inclined to worship the bread and wine itself instead of the dear Saviour if they saw angels bending in worship above it ...." She plunged on almost reckless now, "The fact is, we have a new clerk who comes in now every day and he says – well I hope you won't consider me unorthodox – and he is a venerable old man, Celtic I think, he says that we should not think of it as a sacrifice. He explained it so well to me – says he will not be responsible for misleading people into thinking he is turning the bread and wine into ... into something else like some pagan magician – he says that is the plain meaning of the words of the Holy Scriptures ... Dear Eadwulfu does not like it but I do think it seems sensible. It is a change in the heart that matters, isn't it? I try to teach them but I'm so often ill. Just as I feel I'm making some headway, down I go again. Most of them are here because no one wants them, or they are widows ... All too often I am too ill even to read but I am studying the Scripture more now and I find our clerk is right. I thought you might understand ... "

"I understand completely," I said. "I have a Celtic friend, a man who sometimes has the king's ear. He says the same things as your new clerk."

I wanted to broach the subject of Leofrun with the Abbess but it seemed impossible. How could I explain how I knew anything about her? Nor could I get to the root of the other problem and repeat to the Abbess what I knew of Eadwulfu either.

Then one day, as I was coming in rather tired for my supper, Wynflæd met me at the door full of excitement. "Here!" she said, nodding and winking like some horrible conspirator, "I have something for you!" and she produced a pair of small wax writing tablets – the sort that fold over and are tied together with a little strip of leather. Puzzled, I took them from her and opened them out, thinking perhaps they were some kind of accounts relating to the timber that was supposed to be on its way. It was dark inside Wynflæd's house and I stepped outside to read the scratches on the cool green wax better. To my surprise Wynflæd followed me, positively quivering with nosiness.

"What does she say?" she asked.

"Who? I haven't read it yet, Wynflæd, please move out of the light."

I squinted at the neat handwriting in the late evening sun. "I have prayed as you said," I read. "I have relief for my soul. How could I have been so blind and foolish! I have asked his forgiveness and there is light on every page. I spoke to the Abbess and asked to be given the task of copying the main text and she has set me to work on the Book of the Gospel of John. I drink in the words. Copying is such gloriously slow work and I can meditate on each sentence. Today I reached, '... and shall not be condemned but has passed from death to life.' I thought my heart would burst with joy. Pray for the health of the Abbess; it is my safety."

I thought of Leofrun steadily copying out the words. I knew them so well that they seemed to me now obvious and simple because the heavenly light already lit up that page for me. God had sent his Son to die for sinful men. Believing in him is passing from death to life. This is the best news anyone can ever hear. I could see from her message, that my prayer, and hers, had been answered. True understanding of the words comes when God sends his Holy Spirit to pour, as Leofrun had put it, "light on every page". For her this was the first dawning of that light and it was truly wonderful. And something was dawning in my mind too. How could I have let myself be blinded? How ...

"What does she say?" Wynflæd's voice brought me back to earth with a jolt.

"She says – more or less – that she has been praying and reading God's Word," I replied.

Wynflæd snorted, "Very proper! And the rest I'll be bound. A great many squiggles in that wax for so few words!"

If Wynflæd had been able to read I would certainly not have been the first person to receive the message scratched onto the tablets!

"I'll take your reply, of course," she added, bursting with eagerness.

Wynflæd was thrilled to be passing secret notes between her wood-carver lodger and a young nun but, suddenly, although I was full of joy to hear of Leofrun's new understanding and peace of soul, I was worried. What she was doing in writing to me, however innocent her motive, was dangerous. Wynflæd was a notorious gossip; I could not possibly trust her to carry messages.

I was flustered as I sat down to my supper. How could I reply without putting Leofrun in more danger? That she might not be expecting me to reply at all did not occur to me!

But sleep does amazing things. When I woke the next morning, the answer was buzzing around in my head, displacing all my fears and alarms with the most creative idea I had had since my return to Wessex.

In a corner at the back of the chapel I worked with energy on the next bench end. Gone was my idea of a wild boar. Opposite the cow would be something I had taught myself to carve before I ever left Wessex to study my craft, a dragon. I had had to make up my wolf from my imagination and what I knew of large dogs. But there was no need for imagination when it came to a dragon! I had seen the wicked-looking claws that grace a dragon's feet. I had seen the huge serrated teeth that curved back into its mouth. I had felt its very breath and I needed only my memory to make something truly ferocious. I gave it a mouth that was open, showing off those teeth, and I measured the exact distance between them with care as it was the key to my purpose. I was almost frightened by it myself before I'd finished and I covered it carefully with an old piece of cloth whenever I left it. On the evening of the third day I sat down under the apple tree to compose my reply to Leofrun. When I had finished, I went to find Wynflæd.

"No," I said in response to her excited enquiry, "you do not need to take her the writing tablet. Just tell her, 'a dragon will speak if you touch him under his chin.'"

# Chapter 12
# The Dragon Speaks

At last some of the timber I needed arrived and for several days I was busy overseeing its delivery and sorting it out for the task in hand. It was important that it did not clutter up the chapel which was in constant use so I arranged with the carter to borrow the cart in which it came. The cow and dragon bench was finished now and I had uncovered it and put it in its place with the others. The first thing I did every morning, when the chapel was empty, was to check the dragon's mouth. Would Leofrun have been able to collect the writing tablet?

For days it was still where I had left it, resting between those ferocious teeth. I began to think Wynflæd had muddled the message or that Leofrun had misunderstood it. At night now the robber's nightmare face was mixed up with the dragon's head in hideous contortions as I tossed and turned in my anxiety. Had Leofrun missed the little hole under the dragon's chin into which I had intended her to push her finger, so raising the tablet to slide it easily out from between the teeth? Or was my plan, of creating an animal so fierce the other nuns would avoid it, a failure? Perhaps someone else always took the seat next to it. Had I been too riddling with my message? Wynflæd had never been in the chapel so perhaps I could have been more explicit without her understanding. But she was such a gossip that the message could easily have got out and it was hazardous enough as it was.

Then, one morning, just when I was beginning to give up hope and considering risking passing something via Wynflæd again, the tablet was gone!

Now I was in another agony of suspense. Suppose someone else had found it? Suppose Leofrun had been caught with it? It was hard to carry on working with all these thoughts jigging about in my head. Somehow I managed to carry on with the decorative panels the Abbess had asked for and then, as the time for Terce, the Nuns' mid-morning service, approached, I cleared up everything as usual, ready for the nuns to come and sing the office, and took myself off outside where I could be sure to have a good view of them as they entered the chapel. At least perhaps I could reassure myself that Leofrun was safe and well.

I watched them. Æthelgifu and Eadwulfu led them in through the massive door. I saw Æbbe and her companions, there was old Berta – I scanned the group anxiously – yes, there she was walking quietly behind Berta; that was a relief.

As the nuns' sweet voices soared into the morning air I began to make some plans. I had no idea what would happen next but it occurred to me that I could at least be prepared. I would make sure that ladder I had borrowed was to hand. I would unload my stack of timber near the wall where the old apple tree was and I would have a talk with the carter.

I had made my way to Shaftesbury under the guidance of the glum fyrdman who had come with me. I had no experience of the roads myself and little idea of how, for instance, I would reach the Nun Oswynn's house without a guide. The carter, however, knew the area well and I patiently wheedled out of him some good directions under the pretext of possibly going to inspect some more timber myself before taking delivery of it.

"I have a special project in view," I explained, "and it needs not only the *best* timber but the most *suitable* for the task. It is hard for anyone but myself to judge what I need."

He understood, "I know where you might find timber for sale. It's quite a way from here," he said, "but it is all good seasoned stuff."

"What direction?" I asked. "Beyond the Nun Oswynn's, is it?"

"No, no," he said. "It is in that direction but not so far. You can take a path that leaves the main cart track about a mile out of Shaftesbury and then instead of turning left down the ride to the nun's place, you carry straight on, can't miss it, a big house with barns and sheds full of timber."

By the time we had finished talking, I had a good idea of the route to take if I needed to get Leofrun back to her mother's house in a hurry.

Now I began to check the dragon's mouth regularly in case the writing tablet was returned. Again there was nothing for several days and then something happened that caused me great alarm.

I was in the habit now of standing unobtrusively outside the chapel to watch the nuns make their way in to sing the terce, sext, none and vespers services at their set hours of the day – just to check that Leofrun was still safe. As I watched the nuns approaching for Terce one morning I saw that Æthelgifu was leaning on one of them for support. At sext the same thing happened. At none there was a nun either side of her helping her walk and at vespers she was virtually carried in. This was what Leofrun had feared. What was it she had said? "... Find a way to ... force me ... threatened ... totally ruthless ... Novices do not leave Shaftesbury – they know too much ..." The horrible words rattled round in my head. My first act after the nuns had left the chapel was to run my hand over the dragon's mouth. The writing tablet was back inside!

# Chapter 13
# A Plan

*The dear Abbess is ill. Please pray for her that she will continue to be able to get to the chapel as she loves to do – to sing the offices. I have been told that, under certain circumstances, not I but Berta will be severely punished. I am also forbidden any more to enter the scriptorium. This burden I find hard to bear. I had comfort from the Word of God there. I could do what is needed to protect Berta with a resigned heart if I could have that privilege always. As it is, you talked of help. If there is any, I will gladly take it. Æbbe and some of the others are kinder since the torn cope. They might assist me. Pray for me.*

I dragged the flat side of the stylus over the tablet and the message was gone; the tablet was as innocently blank as if it had never been written.

"Under certain circumstances ..." so Eadwulfu would force Leofrun to take her vows by threatening to harm poor old Berta if she refused! I thought of those greedy little eyes, that hard mouth. I knew Eadwulfu was capable of such scheming cruelty once the Abbess herself was unable to control her. Eadwulfu must have noticed, too, that Leofrun was deriving some sort of comfort and support from her work in the scriptorium which sustained her in her steadfast refusal to comply with Eadwulfu's demand. I wondered if Leofrun had been telling the other nuns about what she had been reading; Eadwulfu would probably dislike that as well. But, in denying Leofrun access to the scriptorium, Eadwulfu was dealing her own plans a death blow. Leofrun's message was clear; she would be prepared to take the vows to protect the old nun if she could continue to have the comfort of God's Word. Facing life without this comfort had driven her to ask for my help to escape. I wondered if Æbbe and her friends would cover for her to give us more time to get away.

Escape! Suddenly it was all too horribly real. Up to now the whole idea had been something almost imaginary. I had mulled over plans and possible routes but always secure in the thought that there would probably never be a real need to use them. I clutched at a straw; how ill was the Abbess? Perhaps she would recover and everything would blow over. Then I discovered something else: part of me definitely did not want Leofrun to remain forever shut away in Shaftesbury Abbey. Deep inside I was as desperate for her to get out as she was. I peered with fascinated horror into my own developing emotions. What I saw almost frightened me. I was preparing to remove a nun from a royal abbey without the king's express permission – preparing to break the law of Wessex. Yet I found I was not ready to give up this dangerous idea.

I went to bed but I tossed and turned again as various unsuitable plans arose in my mind and were discarded. Should I try to get Leofrun over the wall? I had ladders. It would be difficult, especially in the dark. Should I enlist the help of Wynflæd? That would be dangerous and in any case what could she do? Berta would help but it would have to be in a way that would not incriminate her. It was a still night with no wind and mild. Wynflæd's house was stuffy and airless and a stale smell of last night's pottage hung in the air. Faintly, so faintly, the sound of the nuns' matins rose, just audible above Wynflæd's snores. A plan, little better than the others, perhaps, but with some chance of success, nudged its way into my mind and I fell into an exhausted sleep, my mind too worn out even to drag the robber's cruel face before me to keep me awake.

In the morning I went to see the carter. "I urgently need to see that timber we were talking about," I told him. "Can I hire a horse from you? Then I can take the cart and bring back whatever he's got at the same time."

The carter seemed happy with the idea and I arranged to make an early start. "I need to get going well before dawn," I explained. "It's a long way and I shall probably have to spend quite a while looking over what is there before I can decide." He was not to know that I intended to deliver Leofrun back to her mother before looking at any timber! He was only mildly surprised that I wanted to leave at such an hour and when I cheerfully paid him in advance and offered to see to the horse myself without waking him, he readily agreed.

Then I went to see the Abbey porter behind his tiny window. By now he had got used to various supplies coming in for my use and was not surprised at my being so fussy as to want to choose my own timber for such an important project. He was a chatty little man eager for news and gossip so I regaled him with a description of the flying angels I had originally had in mind in a way that would give him several tasty titbits of information, albeit rather out of date now, to share about their intended size, attitude and even facial expression. I did not tell him that I had since discarded these ideas completely.

"Guardians of the Abbey they will be," he said enthusiastically, "spreading their wings over us all."

"We must remember they will be only reminders," I said hastily, "just pictures of the real angels who do God's bidding."

He seemed unable, or unwilling to see the distinction but was happy for me to bring the horse in through his gate and take it out with the cart between matins and lauds, specially when I suggested it could be done without waking him.

"An important errand, fetching the wood for the Abbey's holy guardian angels," he said. "Look, I'll leave the shutter unbolted.

The key is on this hook; you can reach in and take it. There's no one around at that time in the morning. When you've finished, just be sure to lock up and return the key."

The only hurdle now was the town gate itself. I set off to visit the quarter of the town where the fyrd was garrisoned.

When I returned to Wynflæd's, I found her slapping down barley bannocks on her bake-stone in a bad temper. Apparently the Abbess Æthelgifu's illness was making life difficult for her.

"So unreasonable she is that Eadwulfu!" she complained, "always wanting the next thing before you've finished the last job. I told her yesterday, butter won't churn no faster whatever you do to it. You'll have to finish these yourself; if I'm late in the dairy there'll be trouble."

"Doesn't she have to spend most of her time looking after the Abbess?" I asked, for I had rather hoped that Eadwulfu's attention would be taken up with Æthelgifu just at the moment and she would have less time to supervise the nuns.

Wynflæd snorted. "She does no sick nursing – and a good thing for the Abbess that she doesn't too! Would you want to be looked after by her? No, an old woman from the town – a good nurse she is I'll grant you – comes in to care for the Abbess when she's bad."

"Not the nuns?" I was surprised.

"No," said Wynflæd. "She's always keen to keep the Abbess away from the nuns, is Eadwulfu. Of course it's not possible when she's perfectly well but that's not often nowadays. When she's ill like this it is easier to keep her out of it. Eadwulfu prefers to control things herself and at the moment that's just what she's doing." And with that she stomped out into the light drizzle towards the Abbey gate.

# A Plan

I chewed my way meditatively through some warm bannocks. I had plenty to think about. When I had finished I got out the wax tablet.

"Climb into the cart after matins tomorrow," I wrote; this was no time for riddles so I was forced to abandon my usual guarded language, "It is behind the chapel. Cover yourself with the sacking and straw you will find there. God bless you." No point in saying anything else. The less she knew the better if anything went wrong. I had to acknowledge that it would be a huge risk for her to trust me. Perhaps she would not be prepared to take it. Perhaps, when I had gone through it all, she would not be there.

Once the message was inside the dragon's mouth, I knew I had laid my plans as carefully as I could. They seemed frail. That evening, as I squeezed myself into my usual nook behind the apple tree, I prayed earnestly for both of us. Now I no longer prayed my usual prayer over whether or not the Scripture should always be read only in the light of the church's traditions or just on its own. That prayer had already been answered. Now I understood that it was the Scripture and not the tradition that mattered. The tradition could be wrong: Scripture could not. It was a riddle no longer.

I wondered how to keep awake. That afternoon I had tried to snatch a nap but had been fairly unsuccessful. Now that I wanted to be wakeful, my head kept nodding. The drizzle had persisted all day and through the evening. I hoped it would not get worse. I did not relish getting soaking wet as well as committing a crime. Wynflæd's rhythmical snores which had so often kept me awake now seemed like a lullaby so I stood up to stay alert. Would Leofrun trust me? Would she have got my message in any case? Would she have been able to act on it? Would she be there in the cart? There were so many reasons why she would not. The night wore on and I decided the time was about right to go and fetch the carter's horse. By some miracle I had gauged the hour precisely and as

I led him, already harnessed to go between the shafts, up to the gate I heard the sweet sound of matins in the chapel. We waited, the horse and I, in the drizzle until the angelic voices ceased and the sound of footsteps on the gravelled walk died away. Now I no longer felt sleepy. But would she be there? The moon was full but the light was diffused by the drizzly atmosphere into a soft shadowless glow. Would she be there? Everything was perfectly quiet. I felt inside the porter's window. Would she be there? My hand closed over the keys.

It was not possible to get the gate open, get the horse inside and lead him up to the chapel in perfect silence but we were well away from the nuns' dorter or sleeping quarters so there was little danger of being heard. I hitched up to the cart as quietly as I could without even looking inside it. Would she be there? With my heart thumping so that I was sure it would wake the whole of Shaftesbury I said quietly, "Leofrun?"

# Chapter 14
# Escape

"Wulfgar?" The sacks and straw whispered back to me.

"Yes, keep still. Don't move until I tell you." She was there. She trusted me. Suddenly, I was not afraid. As I patted the neck of the carter's horse, my hand trembled not with fear but with suppressed elation.

"Walk on!" I said – so softly – but he understood. We were on our way.

I had left the gate open and we walked through. I locked it behind us and returned the key to its place behind the little window, carefully pulling the unbolted shutter closed.

The drizzle began to lift and the sky cleared. The glorious full moon sailed out from behind the dispersing clouds. We made our way towards the town gate in a blaze of silver moonlight. Behind the locked gate I brought the horse to a standstill and we waited. It seemed like eternity. I strained my ears for the sound of the fyrd watchman to approach on his rounds. Silence. We waited. I was shaking again. When the fyrdman arrived he would wonder what was the matter with me! We waited. Could I hear him coming? Slow measured footsteps. Getting nearer. He could see us now and hailed us with an arm raised in salute.

"Hello, Wood-carver!" he spoke quietly but it sounded deafening, "You're early! When I was told to expect you before dawn I thought they meant just before, not the middle of the night!"

And then I was not shaking. I was calm and relaxed as I held the bridle, "Yes, but I was not asleep and now the rain has stopped so I'll get underway. It's going to be a massive job and the sooner I get off the sooner I'll be back to see the stuff carefully unloaded and stashed away in the dry." And for a moment I had a mental picture of my well-planned return to Shaftesbury later in the day with the timber and without Leofrun. It seemed strangely bleak.

He nodded and began to unlock the gate. "I've heard it's to make us some guardian angels for the Abbey chapel," he said in an awed voice. "No doubt it takes holy timber for that."

I could not explain now, though everything inside me wanted to shout "No!" and instead we trundled through and I thanked him. He saluted again and shut the gate. I heard him barring it behind us. We were outside Shaftesbury.

I hoped Leofrun was not uncomfortable but I dared not even speak to her until we were well clear of the town. The cloud had completely dispersed by now and the moonlight threw sharp shadows. I kept to an easy pace walking beside the cart; forcing myself not to speak or hurry until we had covered what I judged to be about a mile. We were well out of sight of the town and into the woods before I stopped the horse and spoke: "Leofrun?"

Her head popped up from the straw and she was pulling aside the old sacks and coverings I had dumped in the cart. I jumped up onto the cart and shook the reins. Now was the time to make all possible speed while the moonlight held. "Come and sit here," I said. At the bottom of the cart she would be roughly jolted about once the horse was no longer just ambling along. She struggled forward, clutching the jolting side of the cart, and sat beside me pulling straw off her wimple and habit and trying to smooth down her crumpled clothes.

# Escape

"Berta and Æbbe will cover for me," she said. "No one will miss me until after Terce and maybe not even then. I was worried about Berta but she says Eadwulfu won't hurt her once I'm actually gone. There would be no point. They helped me get into the cart, both of them."

Something warned me that I should not ask *how* they would cover for her. The less I knew the better for everyone involved if things went wrong. I concentrated on keeping the horse on the cart track and gradually there was the grey light of dawn.

At length we reached the point where the track to the Nun Oswynn's house led off from the cart road. I stopped the horse and jumped down to look round for a good place to leave the cart where it would not be seen by anyone passing by. The road was bordered by trees but they were not in full leaf. The cart would have to be a long way off the road before it would be well hidden and that would leave obvious traces. There was enough light to see well now and I beat about a bit and found a damp hollow back from the road a little way.

"Jump down," I said to Leofrun, offering her my hand. "This is where the cart will have to stop. It is too slow and very conspicuous and if the road gets narrow, we don't want to have to abandon it in a hurry."

I unhitched the horse and pushed the cart down into the hollow. It was not an easy job and anyone looking closely would see traces. In the hollow itself the ground was deeply muddy and my clothes were soon spattered and my boots caked. I began pulling up bracken and undergrowth from behind the hollow and piling it over the cart to form a screen, shielding my hands inadequately from the brambles with some old sacking. Leofrun saw what I was doing and grabbed some sacking herself, pitching in to help me. The brambles tore at my clothes and face and I smeared off most of the blood with the muddy sacking. We had just finished to my satisfaction when Leofrun grabbed my arm.

## Wulfgar and the Riddle

"Listen!" she hissed. "Someone's coming."

I pushed her down into the brambles behind the cart and scrambled out on to the road. Almost as soon as I did so, three horse men came into view at a brisk trot from the direction in which we had just come. I led the carthorse across to the side of the road where the cart was hidden as if to make a passage for the riders which I hoped they would take without looking too closely. Then I picked up one of his hoofs and began to examine it. The riders drew rein as they approached me and halted. They were fyrdmen and I saw with horror that in charge of the party was the very fellow who had accompanied me from Leofham to Shaftesbury!

He looked me up and down with his usual glum expression and I knew at once that he recognised me, despite my totally dishevelled and mud-stained appearance.

"What have we here, then?" he asked and before I could answer one of the others sniggered, "Someone's run off with a nun from the Abbey – you haven't seen them, have you?"

Still cradling the horse's hoof, I looked up to reply, "I'm looking for a stone." It was all I could think of to say.

The fyrdman in charge looked me up and down again with narrowed eyes, "The king is on his way to Æt Baðum," he said to my surprise, loftily ignoring his subordinate's remark. "Where he will be receiving the submission of King Hyfaidd of Dyfed to his overlordship. We are on our way to meet him with a message from the Abbey regarding a nun who has been abducted. If you hear any news of her, send a message there at once."

I gaped – was he not going to give me away? I nodded stupefied. I think my mouth was hanging open like an idiot's.

"Do you know this fellow?" asked one of the others suddenly.

## Escape

The fyrdman gathered his reins and signalled for them to continue on the cart road, "Do you think I hobnob with vagabonds like that?" I heard him say sharply as they turned to continue their journey.

I watched them, still hoof in hand, until they were well out of sight. Then I went to find Leofrun. She had overheard every word and for the first time she seemed frightened. But there was no time even for fear. We must get to Oswynn's before anyone else caught up with us. I hoisted her, as muddy as myself and her habit the worse for its encounter with the brambles, up onto the back of the horse. Then I got up in front of her and turned him onto the track into the woods.

For a long time we made our way along the narrow path in silence. Leofrun's mood had changed completely. I could not really see her, of course, but I knew, as the horse made his way through the twists and turns, that she was crying quietly.

"What's the matter?" I asked, stupidly. After what she had been through in the last few hours it would be surprising if she were not crying. There was no answer. I tried again, "Not so far now to your mother's house." I said it encouragingly, although I was well aware that she knew where we were better than I did. There was still no answer so I gave it up and concentrated on the horse.

Suddenly she said, "I didn't realise what you ... what I was doing."

"What do you mean?" I asked, puzzled.

"They said ... that fyrdman – he was a fyrdman, wasn't he? – that you have *abducted* me – 'run off with a nun,' he said, the other one," she shuddered, "and he was laughing about it."

My arms holding the reins went stiff and under the mud stains my face reddened with embarrassment. Before I could say anything, she asked, "It's not true, is it? Not like that?"

I hesitated, "You asked me to help you get out ... you were being forced into taking those vows ... that's all ... "

She was quiet. Once more, I made myself think of what might happen if things went wrong. "Leofrun," I said, "if all this does not work out, if they catch up with us, that's what they'll think has happened. If you can do it without being untruthful, don't contradict them. Let them think I ... I did carry you off – against your will. You'll be safer that way and, who knows, you might still be able to get back to your mother."

There was a long shuddering sob from behind me. "And let you take the blame," she asked, "for ... for doing that?"

"They'll blame me for it anyway, whatever you say," I replied. "It won't make any difference. But this is not the way to talk! We're not far from safety now and we are not caught yet. You probably need something to eat. I always find I feel low when I'm hungry. I should've got some barley bannocks from Wynflæd – they're good her bannocks."

"I've got some bannocks and some cheese."

"Excellent! Have a bite to eat then if you can manage it."

There was a bit of rummaging behind me and then she was tucking into something.

The sun rose high in the sky and the woods gave way to more open farm land. I urged the horse to more speed. I was not keen to pass through villages because I knew if anyone was looking for us they would soon know that we were ahead of them. But there was nothing for it. We passed peasants dibbing beans and peas into the ground with sticks, a ploughman and his team, some men sowing barley. They all hailed us as we passed and I felt conspicuous. True, Leofrun's habit was so filthy and torn it was hardly recognisable for what it was but that was hardly a disguise.

If a party of fyrdmen asked them, they would be sure to say they had seen us and give a description.

I was glad to bid goodbye to the last of the hard-working peasants as the path plunged back into the woods. After my recent experience of travelling in the forest I never imagined I would feel safer there than out in the open but as we entered the trees I felt only relief. The way became more difficult and we had to go more slowly again. And all this time we had hardly said a word to each other. I never felt less like a dashing rescuer in my life. She had not exactly trusted me after all. She just hadn't realised what she was doing. Now she did realise, she was mortified. But I did not have to endure these unhappy reflections much longer.

Midday. For miles now, I had been glancing warily behind me every so often but there was no sign of pursuit and I began to grow more confident. I could not believe it had been so easy. I relaxed a little mentally. Perhaps when this was all over and sorted out I could return to Leofham Burgh. Then I would tell Morcant what I had learned, how I had solved the riddle, through Leofrun's experiences – and my own. When you were in difficulties, when someone really needed help, the Scripture was the place to turn. And the best, the only, way to understand it was to study the plain meaning of the words themselves. I pictured myself explaining to him and watching his face as he heard of my change of heart. Then suddenly my reverie was broken. The road came out onto a sort of ridge-way and below us we could see more peasants working in the fields.

"My mother's land! God be praised!" said Leofrun fervently.

I urged the horse forward and we descended into a little belt of trees and then out into the fields again. I could see the women now, they were dibbing beans or peas into the ground, and surely that was Adam with them! I hailed him joyfully, "Adam, Adam!" and waved my arms, urging the horse to a brisk trot.

There was no time for long explanations. "Get her to her mother," I said to the startled clerk as we rode up and I helped Leofrun dismount. "She'll tell you herself what it's all about. There's no time to lose. The fyrd are after us and if we are caught she'll be taken back to Shaftesbury before she's had a chance to speak to her. We ... "

Leofrun gave a cry and pointed. On the distant skyline, where the path followed the ridge, was a party of riders.

"Hide her! As you serve God, man!" I cried desperately to Adam, although where on earth he could do it I had no idea. "I'll draw them off – quick!"

Adam was a fast thinker. As I mounted the horse I could see him marshalling Leofrun into the line of pea-planting women. One of them threw her own old sacking apron over Leofrun's grubby habit. I turned into the path and urged the horse forward. They would catch me but if I could just lure them far enough away first ...

# Chapter 15
# Caught!

"Get down off that stolen horse!"

"It's him sure enough!"

"Robbers who attack travellers in broad daylight and now nun-stealers! Wessex is just not safe these days!"

"Where is she? What have you done with her?"

There were four of them. It had not taken them long to catch up with me. Having spotted me, they rode as hard as they could straight past Adam and the peasant women. They could have had no inkling of where Leofrun was.

A draft horse with no proper saddle is no match for a party of well-mounted young fyrdmen. Gradually the distance between us had decreased and they overhauled me, forcing the carthorse to a stop. It turned out they had been more thorough than the earlier fyrdmen and had found the abandoned cart. But although they were thorough, they did not seem particularly bright. They were young – raw recruits almost I judged them to be – and there was no officer in charge of them. (They had no acquaintance of mine who had also been entertained generously by the Nun Oswynn with them either.) It never seemed to occur to them that Leofrun could be hiding nearby and they assumed that, since I was riding alone when they spotted me, I must have been alone for some time. When, in answer to their barrage of questions, I told them my name, they were triumphant.

"That's him! That's the name we were told in the message from Shaftesbury!"

"Where is the nun, you evil thief?"

I remained resolutely silent on Leofrun's whereabouts so they began to form their own opinions.

"Dead in some ditch like as not, you murderer! Where is she?"

"You'll answer for this!"

"He's killed her – just look at him!"

It was true that I did not present an encouraging appearance. My face was streaked with mud and, what was worse, caked blood from the bramble scratches.

"Aye, yes, he looks like an unholy criminal. Just like that robber we picked up yesterday!"

"A vile creature like this would be capable of any sacrilege!"

"We should put him to death ourselves for killing a nun! Look, he does not deserve a trial, the villain!"

Although this idea clearly appealed to them, they did not quite have the courage to carry it out without orders, I am glad to say. They contented themselves with trussing me up efficiently enough and dumping me back on the horse which they tied to a leading rein. Then they set off, with me in tow, for Æt Baðum.

I would dearly love to forget that gruelling journey and I will not go into details of it here. All I will tell you is that by the time we reached Æt Baðum the young fyrdmen had convinced themselves that they had managed to apprehend the most dangerous ruffian at large in Wessex. By now firm in their conviction that I must have killed Leofrun somewhere on the road, they reasoned that I

## Caught!

must also have committed many other horrible crimes. Since I was known to have recently been working in the Abbey at Shaftesbury they employed their time on the road theorising about what grisly deeds I could therefore have committed there. By the time they had finished their wild speculations they had convinced themselves that it was more than likely there was not a single nun left alive in the place.

When we arrived at Æt Baðum the town was teeming with people and more were constantly arriving from all over Wessex, Mercia and from Wales. The place was so packed that it was difficult to imagine that there was anyone who was *not* there. From the fyrdmen's conversation I had gathered that Prince Hyfaidd of Dyfed was expected to arrive at any moment. Aethelred, Lord of the Mercians, had already arrived for the ceremony along with the Mercian Bishop of Worcester. The place was swarming with fyrdmen, the king's thanes with their attendants, blacksmiths, tinsmiths, armourers, masons, Welsh followers of Hyfaidd in advance of their prince, Aethelred's thanes and attendants as well as the bishop's retinue, everyone busy and hurrying about their duties.

The ancient town of Æt Baðum lies on the border between Wessex and Mercia. A wooden stockade, like that round Leofham Burgh, had been newly built round the town to protect it. Inside this new defence, the old stone walls, which had been allowed to decay since the days of the "giants," were being repaired in safety. Dressed and prepared stone was being hauled from the disintegrating old buildings to fill the gaps and raise the fallen sections. The king's court was held in a building beside the great hot baths which were still the town's main feature. Although the once magnificent bath buildings were in sad disrepair, the hot healing water still bubbled up from the earth as it had always done. In Francia, the great Emperor Charlemagne might have built his magnificent court at Aachen from similar ruined pagan buildings at a hot spring, but somehow, here in Wessex, the crumbling remains of *our* natural hot baths had never been restored. I wondered what on earth poor Brother Grifo had thought of the place!

Tired and in pain (they were not gentle, those fyrdmen) I was in no condition to notice much of these surroundings at the time. I was handed over to a fyrd captain who plainly had no idea where to put me and eventually I was chained up in part of a completely ruined and almost roofless building near the barracks. There I was to remain until it could be determined whether I should be brought before the king. I thought of those piercing, intelligent eyes and I knew that if I could tell him the *whole* story he would believe me. I prayed earnestly that I *would* be able to speak to the king. But in such grim circumstances it was hard even to pray. I tried to remember that Leofrun was safe with her mother and that that was what mattered – but I will not recount more of my misery. Enough to say that utter weariness eventually overcame fear and pain and I slipped into some kind of sleep – but not for long.

I think it was the sound of the door banging shut and someone jangling keys that woke me and for a moment I was utterly confused as to where I was. The vile face of my nightmares was staring down at me. The piercing dark eyes, the savage wild expression burnt brown by the sun and wind and hardened by a thousand evil deeds – would it never stop haunting me? Why would that face not go away when I opened my eyes? There was a groan and a curse. That hoarse rasping voice! Now I was trembling all over. This was real! The light of dawn was streaming in through the broken roof. I was a prisoner chained up in Æt Baðum and chained beside me, leaning over me was the robber whose hideous face had disturbed my sleep for so long.

"What ... who ... how do you come to be here?" I stammered out.

"Through robbing you," he snarled, "I know who you are! Those tools! All marked with your sign. They were on the look out for them, those young pups from the fyrd, and now I'm caught. A bad end to a bad life."

My mind was in a whirl and I stammered out the first thing that came into my head, "Not the ... the end, surely? It is not death for stealing!"

"Might as well be," he growled, "how can I pay back what I owe and that twice over!"

I was trying to think of an answer when there was the sound of a key in the door again, bringing us a visitor, an old monk from the Abbey. He was rather nervous about approaching us – I don't know what he had been told about us but it was plainly intimidating. However, finding me in such a weak and exhausted condition and the robber seemingly not much better, he plucked up courage and explained that he had come from the Abbey almoner to bring us some food. I received mine gratefully and wolfed down the coarse cold barley porridge while he stood and watched us. Gradually I stopped trembling. The robber too was evidently famished and finished his porridge even before I did.

"Not much hope for me, eh?" he asked.

"My son, confess your sins and trust yourself to God," said the monk gravely.

The robber spat. "No help there," he growled.

The edge was off my appetite now and I tried to turn my attention to my own plight.

"Please give my good thanks to your kind almoner who does not forget poor prisoners," I began and I was indeed grateful. "Is the king lodged at the Abbey?" I thought perhaps I could ask this monk to take a message to the Abbot and get a hearing for myself.

"No," he replied, "although Bishop Werferth from Mercia is there."

A bishop was not what I needed so I tried another question.

"I suppose you do not have any news of what will happen to me?"

"Did you not know?" he asked in a tone of surprise, "in spite of all his other business, the king has commanded you before him today. Since it is his daughter who is the Abbess of Shaftesbury he is greatly concerned. My son, you are in an evil case. Murder is a heinous crime and to murder a nun and a nun of a royal foundation where the Abbess herself is the king's daughter ... " He stopped, obviously surprised at the relief on my face at hearing this news.

"Praise the Lord, good brother," I said, "all I ask is to be brought before my king."

# Chapter 16
# The King

As the key turned in the door of our makeshift prison the robber looked at me in astonishment.

"*You* haven't killed a nun, surely," he was almost sneering, "you haven't got it in you! Even I've never killed a clerk – man or woman – but you ...!"

"No, I haven't," I said simply and before I knew where I was I had told him the whole story, even down to telling him how Leofrun had discovered the precious truth that salvation and peace was to be found in the Scripture. To my surprise he listened to everything without a word.

"So I've got to be able to read, have I, to save myself from Hell?" was his astounding comment when I'd finished and there was less of a sneer in his voice, I thought, this time.

"No, no," I assured him. "If you recognise yourself as a sinner ... "

"Pretty obvious that!" he grunted.

"... and repent and come to the Saviour for forgiveness, he will pardon you and give you strength to forsake your old ways."

"And what penance would I have to do?"

"Penance?"

## Wulfgar and the Riddle

"Yes, to atone for what I've done – done all my life. Walking backwards to Rome with my eyes closed three or four times sounds about right." The sneering note was definitely back again now.

"You can't atone for your own sin, only Christ can atone for you – plead with him!" I urged, "if, as you say, you may lose your life over this affair ... "

"Not if I can help it," he muttered.

"... if you may lose your life, there is no time to waste!"

We talked on. He seemed to veer between real concern for his soul one moment and hopeless sarcasm the next. I would dearly have loved to be able to give him some part of the Scripture written down but alas, even if I had had such a thing to spare, he would not have been able to read it. Again I thought of Brother Grifo's unthinking remark that had caused me such heart-searching, "How is the church to retain its power over the people if they think they can understand God's teaching for themselves?" What an ill thing it was in reality to have an illiterate peasantry and so few Bibles! If only the king's plans for more widespread reading would come to fruition!

At length, a couple of fyrdmen unlocked the door and hauled me out and onto my feet. "Farewell!" I shouted, "and remember what I've been trying to tell you!" and, to my surprise, as the door banged shut, I heard him call in reply, "I'll do that!" Nor was there any hint of sarcasm in his tone.

Beside the old baths was a building in far less disrepair than most of the tumbledown old ruins in Æt Baðum. Over the doorway fluttered the standard of Wessex, the golden wyvern, and beside it stood two fyrdmen on guard duty. I was hustled through the crowds by one of the fyrdmen who had fetched me from my prison quarters and into the magnificent hall. The robber was left behind and all thoughts of him were, for the moment, swept from my mind. The room was lined with important-looking people but there was an open space before the dais which was richly hung with embroidered tapestries. For a split second I thought of Berta and her companions and it flashed across my mind that I had never considered the sad human cost of such finery before. The king was flanked by nobles and churchmen with whom he was in earnest conversation. To my great joy and amazement there was someone else on the dais whom I knew well. Sitting next to a scholarly looking monk was – Morcant! Of course! He had told me that the king had summoned him for Prince Hyfaidd's submission and here he was!

Even if he saw me, Morcant did not recognise me. Despite my attempts to clean myself up I was still a scruffy half-shaven wretch but I waited with growing confidence to be called before the king.

In front of the dais was a floor of breath-taking beauty, the rival of anything I had seen in Francia, paved with pictures of sea creatures – dolphins and hippocampi – all made out of thousands of tiny pieces of coloured stone. Across this the king's noble and energetic voice rang clearly.

"Brother Asser," he was saying to the monk sitting next to Morcant, "I have need at my court for men of learning such as you. Bishop Werferth here will tell you of the translation projects I have on hand. Stay here with us! I will ask Prince Hyfaidd to excuse you from returning to Dyfed and he will not refuse me. Morcant of Tyddewi here has ... er ... vowed to remain at Leofham Burgh or I would have recruited him years ago."

I could not hear the monk's reply but then the king was speaking again. "Then divide your time between my court and Dyfed if you will – but I will give you space to consider."

Now a messenger was speaking to the king but again I could not hear his words. "At last!" said the king, "now perhaps we can get to the bottom of this strange message from my daughter's Abbey!" He consulted a wax tablet before him, "'... a workman ... stolen some bannocks, some cheese, a cart, and a horse and abducted a nun from Shaftesbury ... without the king's permission ... .' It is sealed with my daughter's seal and yet it is strange – the message does not read like something from her gracious hand at all. Where is this villain that has been apprehended? Have him brought forward."

I was pushed to the front by the fyrdman and I fell on my knees before the dais. The last time I had been in this position before my king I had received great and generous kindness from him but I confess I was frightened. What I had done would take some explaining and the king might simply not have time to listen to it all.

"You have stolen bannocks, cheese, a cart and a horse and abducted a nun from the Abbey ... " The piercing eyes were scouring my face now, and the king's stern expression changed to one of angry amazement. "But this is Wulfgar! Wulfgar? What on earth? These are extremely serous charges! Surely, you must know that removing a nun from Shaftesbury Abbey without my express royal permission is against the law of the Kingdom of Wessex! I have been patient with you in the past – but this!"

Morcant was on his feet now, staring at me in horrified surprise.

But before anyone could say anything further there was a commotion at the back of the hall. A messenger was pushing his way forward calling out as he came, "Urgent messages for my Lord the King from the Lady Æthelgifu, Abbess of Shaftesbury!"

"Make way!" said the king quickly and as the messenger approached I could see that he too had wax writing tablets in his hand. The king broke the seal that fastened the tablets closed.

"... Trustworthy ... returned a homesick novice to her mother ..."

## The King

I heard him read, "... commendable. I beg you to ignore ... during my illness ... " He put the tablet down carefully. "I think, Wulfgar, that perhaps you have some explaining to do," he said.

It took all my reserves of tact to explain to the king what had happened, without telling him outright that the Lady Æthelgifu, due to her illness, was not always in charge at Shaftesbury and that the Nun Eadwulfu who usurped her position whenever possible, was, to say the least, unsuitable. It was not my place to comment on such matters, nor would it help. I was just beginning to make things fairly clear, emphasising that it was indeed a novice that was involved, when there was a further commotion at the back of the hall and another messenger strode forward carrying yet more wax tablets and stood beside me in front of the king. It was Adam! How on earth had he got an audience?

A fyrdman stepped forward ready to remove the intruder and I'm sure Adam, a mere thrall, and on no known royal business, would have been curtly sent back without delivering his message at all if it had not been for the Celtic monk, John Asser. He leaned across to the king, speaking quietly. Then at a sign from the king he left the dais and took Adam aside to talk to him.

"O, my Lord the King," I said, "please, of your grace, look at this man's messages. He is the servant of the Nun Oswynn, whose daughter is at the centre of this whole business!"

"Wulfgar, I have heard enough of this matter," said the king, quite irritated now by all the interruptions. "John Asser evidently knows this thrall – or knew his father at any rate – go and get yourself cleaned up. It is clear that something needs investigating at Shaftesbury and I am minded to send Asser himself there, since he takes an interest, to find out what on earth is going on. What *is* clear, however, from what my daughter writes, is that no nun has been taken from the Abbey. A *novice* is not a *nun* and may be removed by her family or their agents. I cannot think what you have been doing – all this rubbish about bannocks and cheese and horses and carts – but I will have someone investigate and if you are in the wrong by so much as a hair's breadth, be sure you will be punished with the full weight of the law. Now go."

I stumbled out of the court and into the crowded street. The fyrdman who had been in charge of me vanished. What should I do now? I tried to get out of the crowds although I had no idea where to go. I was also hungry; the barley porridge had not been sustaining. I turned down a broken down side street where things seemed more quiet.

I had not given the horse and cart any thought before. If things had gone according to plan, I had been intending to carry on with the projected trip to the timber merchant and return the horse and cart exactly as promised; I had had no intention of stealing them! How far, far away and long ago it all seemed now! Surely I could not be responsible for theft just because Leofrun had brought her dinner along with her! Why, the cheese was probably some of that cheese I'd carried to Shaftesbury from Leofrun's mother anyway! Spiteful Eadwulfu had just trumped up everything she could think of to charge me with. And then there was Morcant. He was plainly horrified at what I had done. I had been longing to tell him that I had changed my mind. I had been happily anticipating explaining to him how I could see it now, the Word of God, the plain words of Scripture – without any glosses or fancy allegories – was what everyone needed and that if what was in the Scripture was different from church practice and belief then the church needed to return to the Scripture. But that cheerful picture had faded away; Morcant would not want anything to do with me now.

Moodily I kicked at a loose stone from the broken paving and it skidded away in front of me. A dog, no more than a puppy, shot out from a side lane after the stone, chasing it, worrying it and rolling over with it in the dust. "Hey, come here Cyng!" came a shout but the puppy hardly paused. The shout was renewed and round the corner came ... Swefred, dog leash in hand!

## The King

Swefred! I was overwhelmed with thankfulness to find someone I not only knew but could talk to. "Swefred," I shouted eagerly, "O, Swefred, is it really you?"

"Wulfgar!" he exclaimed joyfully. "Absolutely everyone is here in this town! Man! What's happened to you? You could do with a clean up! Thank goodness there's plenty of hot water in this place! Here come with me. I'll ... hey, what's the matter?"

I am not given to tears. I discovered as quite a small child that crying never improves anything. You only have to stop and then the problems, whatever they are, are still there. But I was utterly exhausted with all I had been through, flight, capture, imprisonment, trial, and no definite acquittal – not to mention the reappearance of the robber. The sight of my old friend was more than I could bear. I shook my head, too full of misery to speak.

Swefred's long arm shot out, capturing the errant Cyng and clipping him neatly onto the leash beside a second identical animal. Then he gripped my shoulder, shook it and said, "Look here, bear up, Wulfgar, whatever it is I'm sure Morcant will be pleased to see you. He's ... " There was a sudden shout and the sound of cheering, "That'll be the Welsh prince arriving! These wolfhound pups are a present to him from King Alfred. Come on! I'm supposed to be there. Prince Hyfaidd'll be amazed to see Morcant! Come with me or we'll never find each other again in this crowd." And with that he propelled me, along with the dogs, back towards the king's hall.

The crowd was forming into an avenue from the gates to the hall, the fyrdmen holding them back to give the Welsh royal party a clear path. Swefred marched us both boldly up to the very door of the hall ready to present his gifts. Morcant stood in the shadow of the doorway awaiting the arrival of the prince.

"Look who's here!" Swefred whispered to him excitedly as he pulled the wriggling puppies to a sit. "It's Wulfgar!"

"I've seen him already," replied Morcant grimly, "and once is enough."

But now Prince Hyfaidd was riding through the gates, followed by his colourful retinue and the cheering was redoubled. I caught sight of a short man who rode with easy grace up the avenue of excited crowds, a hand raised to acknowledge their welcome. When he reached the doorway, I got a better view of a stern, hard, battle-scarred face and then Morcant stepped forward from the shadows and held his stirrup for him to dismount. There was a sudden silence, almost as if the crowd had been waiting for this emotional moment. The prince looked down at Morcant for an instant as he dismounted and then broke into a torrent of his native tongue, "*Morcant Tyddewi! Ai chi ydi o go iawn? Ond roeddem yn swr eich bod wedi eich ladd flynyddoedd yn ôl. Beth dych chi'n wneud fan hyn?* – Morcant of Tyddewi! Is it really you? But we were sure you were killed years ago! What are you doing here?" He threw his arms round Morcant, "*yn ôl o'r bedd – O fy ffrind annwyl –* back from the grave – O my dear friend!" and then the two of them were weeping together for joy and all thoughts of solemn ceremony ceased for the moment. Then the crowd was cheering again, Swefred was kneeling with his royal gift of hunting dogs and then the prince passed into the hall with Morcant; a Welsh nobleman leading the leashed dogs walking behind him.

# Chapter 17
# Adam

"It seems to me," said Swefred, "that the first thing we must do is find this Adam of yours."

We were sitting together on some stones in the corner of a shabby building near the barracks. The fyrdmen were using the rest of the room to store weapons and gear but Swefred had been assigned this one corner to himself on account of the royal dogs. He had blown the hearth-fire into life, swinging the iron pot in place over it, and soon I was devouring good hot pottage. Between mouthfuls I managed to tell him the whole story. There was no need to leave out the bits about Eadwulfu with him.

"I don't know how you'd find anyone in this crush of people," I said, when he suggested getting hold of Adam.

"You say he went off with John Asser," replied Swefred, "that makes it easier. Morcant knew Asser before he came to Wessex – they are old friends."

"I'm not sure Morcant will want anything to do with me," I said sadly. "I'm by no means in the clear. The king was angry. It will take more than some message from a thrall from nowhere like Adam to sort things out. The king is a busy man and this is just a small crime in his eyes now – some bread, cheese, a cart and a horse – not something he'll want to deal with personally as it would have been if Leofrun had really been more than just a novice nun."

Wulfgar and the Riddle

"Morcant will understand," said Swefred cheerfully. "He's just not heard the important details, that's all. You know Morcant, he's fair and patient, he'll understand you've done nothing really wrong. Now, let's get you presentable," and with that he picked up a bucket and disappeared on some errand that took just long enough for me to begin to comfortably digest my meal. I was starting to feel much more hopeful (it is amazing what food does for you!) when he returned with his bucket full of something that was steaming gently.

"Here you are," he said, pouring some of the bucket's contents into a cracked bowl, "now you can have a good wash."

I sniffed at the bowl. "Smells like eggs – and none too fresh," I said warily.

"Never mind the smell – it's good stuff," said Swefred starting to wash up our supper things in the bucket. "People come here just to drink it!"

I did my best and then Swefred produced a comb of sorts and brushed down my tunic with something I suspected he usually used on his dogs.

"That's better," he said approvingly when we'd finished, "you look quite human! Now come with me and we'll see if Morcant's finished exchanging news with Prince Hyfaidd."

"Where is Morcant staying?" I asked, "I hope it's somewhere better than this!"

"Oh, he's staying in the Abbey," said Swefred. "They all know me there and I'm welcome – so long as I leave the dogs outside! Morcant spends most of his time in that scriptorium place where all the books are. However, I'm sorry to say the Abbey buildings are in about as bad a state of repair as this place! The old Abbey was only partly built of stone from the ancient buildings and when the Vikings came they torched all the wooden parts. Repairs are underway now but it is by no means finished."

The Abbey was indeed rather a sorry sight. Makeshift buildings of wood and wattle stood around the stone Abbey church, some even leaning against its walls for support. The burnt-out remains of their predecessors were still clearly visible and it gave me a sick feeling to think of the Vikings looting and burning, carrying off books and costly furnishings while the flames licked away at the monks' dortors, workshops and storehouses. I had seen Vikings in action and I could picture what it must have looked like – in fact it was hard to force my mind off it.

When Swefred rapped on the Abbey door, who should open it but my old friend Brother Grifo from Francia! It took a moment for him to recognise me but when he did he was far too well mannered to show his surprise at my scruffy condition. "Wulfgar," he cried, "this is indeed a pleasure! How do you come to be in these parts?"

When I explained that I needed to see Morcant he took my arm and drew us along the corridor towards the scriptorium saying, "You know, you were the only person who warned me what things were like here in Wessex! I would never have imagined such dangerous ideas could have a hold on even quite sensible people. No wonder your noble king is calling out for more scholars!"

I smiled, wondering how to tell him just how much I had changed my mind since I last saw him.

Hasty wooden construction or not, the scriptorium was full of stout shelves and reading desks. When we entered, Morcant was standing poring over a great volume with – Adam, of course! He was in his element.

"... ond ydych chi wedi gweld hyn yn Rhufeniaid? Mae'r ysgrythur yn glir am y pwnc yma dwi'n meddwl... ffydd ydy'r peth pwysig...

but have you seen this in Romans? The Scripture is clear on this subject I think ... faith is the important thing ... "

"*mae'n wir ...* it's true ... *yr un peth yn Corinthiaid hefyd,* the same thing in Corinthians too, *wel, yr holl Feibl i gyd yn dweud bod ...* "

"Morcant," said Swefred quietly as Brother Grifo bowed deferentially and returned to his duties, "sorry to interrupt but I've brought Wulfgar ..."

"Wulfgar!" exclaimed Morcant. "The very person I wanted to see – but I had no idea where you were among all these crowds of people! Adam here ... he's explained everything ... John Asser's looking into it right away! I'm so sorry! I never realised for a moment what had been going on! Please forgive me!"

"I'm not surprised you didn't know what's been going on," I said, "I'm not sure I know myself! But it is clear I owe some thanks to the almoner of this place at any rate; he took the trouble to send us some porridge. I think I'd have died of starvation if it hadn't been for that! Did you know they had captured the robber who took my tools and my money, Morcant? He was chained up with me."

"I did know," said Morcant, "and what you don't know is that he is chained up no longer!"

"Why?" I gasped. "Was he pardoned?"

"No, he was not," said Morcant. "He managed to get free of his chain. Then when the almoner's assistant came to visit him again to feed him and tell him of the danger of his soul, he pushed him aside and made a run for it."

"They did not catch him then? I suppose in all these crowds ... "

"By the time the alarm was raised," said Morcant "he'd

vanished; probably slipped out of the gate in the crowds leaving after Prince Hyfaidd's submission to the king."

"So he's on the loose again," I mused. Yet somehow I was not so sorry as I would have expected. "You know, Morcant, he was asking me about his soul; what kind of ... er ... penance he would have to do if he repented of his sin. He was astounded when I said Christ's forgiveness was freely given. He spared my life, you know, Morcant, I would have thought it a pity if he were to lose his over a few tools and a little gold."

"Maybe," said Morcant, "but consider the danger he is to other travellers. The king is right to clear the roads of such characters."

"I wish people like him could hear the gospel," I said. "They cannot read and there are no copies of the Scripture for them to study if they could."

Morcant nodded and I could see he agreed but then he changed the subject abruptly,"Look at this, Wulfgar!" he said, "their own copy of Ratramnus' *De Corpore et Sanguine Domini* the very treatise Mariwig sent me and – wary as I am of commentaries, I am eager to read this one – Bishop Claudius of Turin on *Genesis*! This place is a treasure-house."

The mention of Ratramnus and Claudius brought the whole issue flooding back to my mind. At last I could tell Morcant what I had been longing to say. "Morcant, I owe you an apology: you were absolutely right. The church is going astray and it is a lack of reading the Scriptures *just as they are* that is causing it. I've been praying and thinking and longing to do some reading myself – reading the *plain words* of the Holy Scriptures! As a result I've acquired a taste for doing plain woodwork too, rather than making things people are tempted to worship! You showed me that Hrypa needed no rood before his eyes to help him understand and nor does anyone else; I see it now."

Morcant's face showed the pleased reaction I had anticipated but all he said was, "Hrypa is a good Christian teacher in his own way."

"But, Morcant," I went on, "now I know this, everything feels so dark. The truth of the gospel itself is getting buried under all this ritual and idolatry. The Scripture is not there for the common people, let alone robbers, in a language they can understand. And if it were, they could not read it for themselves. Those who do have the Scripture seem to twist and darken it with their traditions and refuse to see its plain meaning. The church is becoming nothing more than a structure for climbing to positions of power and wealth while the common people sink back into superstition. It feels as if there will be nothing left of Christianity – as if paganism is creeping back in a Christian dress."

"But we do still have the Scriptures," said Morcant, "and God will not let the light be smothered completely. It may seem dark now but one day the light will flame out again brighter than ever. And meanwhile in every generation there will be a Ratramnus or a Claudius somewhere."

" ... and a Morcant, or an Adam – or even a Mariwig, perhaps," I said, taking courage from his words.

" ... and God will not let his church fail." said Morcant. "Perhaps, for instance, when the king's plans come to fruition and Wessex is no longer beset by the Vikings he will be able to carry out his idea of having as many of his subjects as possible learn to read in the Anglo-Saxon tongue. It may not reach down as far as robbers, at least to begin with, but I know he longs to restore his realm to the state it once enjoyed in that golden age before the Viking raiders began to harry the land. In those days learning was widespread and Latin was commonly understood so Scripture – pure Scripture – was not difficult to read. If he succeeds perhaps then the light will dawn in all its brightness again. But if not, if we have to wait even for centuries in the shadows, it will not be without hope for it is *certain* the true light will one day burst out again."

There was a quiet "Amen," from behind me and I turned round, startled to find some of the monks, who had slipped in silently on their bare feet, listening in quiet agreement.

"The king himself would say the same, Master Morcant," said one.

"Yet he wastes his time on translations of Pope Gregory and the pagan Boethius into Anglo-Saxon instead of concentrating on the pure Word of God!" exclaimed another.

Adam was smiling now. "You see, Wulfgar," he said, "there are more Anglo-Saxons who cherish the Scriptures than you might think."

I remembered my conversation with the Abbess of Shaftesbury, "There are other people who are concerned too! The Abbess Æthelgifu – you only have to talk to her privately to see she is groping towards the same light of Scripture too."

"Yes," said Morcant, "so I must be content to dwell quietly at Leofham Burgh and wait God's good time. Even the orders of a king cannot stop God's work going forward. Confining a plain ordinary clerk like me to Leofham Burgh will not prevent the darkness lifting in God's good time."

"The king has not granted you your freedom, then?" I asked.

"No," replied Morcant, "I am to return tomorrow, but, like Adam here, I am still God's free man."

"He would be welcome here with us," said one of the monks, "but alas, the king will not allow him to stay."

"I need to talk to you, Wulfgar," said Adam, coming down to

earth suddenly. "I've given John Asser and Morcant here all the details frankly, including those you did not mention to the king, and the Nun Oswynn's message makes everything plain as far as her daughter is concerned. Leofrun explained clearly that you had borrowed the horse and cart by arrangement with the owner with every intention of returning them so my mistress has sent one of our best horses in exchange and arranged for the cart to be returned too: that's all settled. She's also sent payment to the Abbey for the bannocks that Leofrun ate – ridiculous as it is, the whole business! I'm afraid she flatly refused to pay for the cheese – she said it was her own in any case!"

A weight fell from my shoulders, "Did you really tell them about Eadwulfu?" I asked, "I just did not dare to go into all that before the king; it would have sounded so churlish – as if I was exaggerating things just to get off – but it is serious."

"Yes, I did," said Adam. "My mistress was indignant at what her daughter told her. She insisted that the king hear the whole story of what is going on – and I think it is for the best. It took us some time to find out where the king was or I would have been here sooner but I think she would have sent me to the ends of the earth if need be, though I'm glad the king turned out to be much nearer than that! I told her I had my doubts about being able to speak to the king in person, but I promised to try. There must always be hundreds of people who want to speak to him about one thing or another and I am nobody," his hand went to his thrall collar as he spoke, "but I will be able to tell her when I return that I have at least laid the whole matter before one of his most trusted churchmen."

"That collar is your royal badge of office, Adam," said Morcant. "You need never to be ashamed of it. The Apostle tells us we are all one in Christ whether bond or free."

"*Yn Galatiaid ...* " murmured Adam.

"Yes, in *Galatians* and in *Corinthians* too," continued Morcant. "But, Adam, it is the goodness of God that it was Asser that was with the king and that he recognised you! He is an ideal man to go into such a matter. He has the king's ear and he can be trusted to sort out any irregularity such as has been going on at Shaftesbury."

"However did you get into the royal court, Adam?" I asked, "I can't imagine how you did it."

"I just told them I came from the mother of the young nun that they were saying was dead and that she was alive," Adam replied. "Someone said, 'You mean she's come back to life from the dead? A miracle! A miracle!' and they were so excited that before I could explain what I meant they were pushing me through the crowds and up to the dais! And I've got something for you too, Wulfgar," he added, pulling yet more sealed wax tablets out of his jerkin. "This is for you from my Mistress, and this from her daughter."

I broke the seal on Oswynn's message first, while Morcant and Adam returned to their happy discussion of the Apostle Paul's letters. After a brief and optimistic opening sentence about the likely outcome of Adam's encounter with the king on my behalf, the rest of the tablet was filled up with a description of Leofrun's many and varied domestic accomplishments. I found this puzzling at first.

Then I opened the seal on Leofrun's message. Why was my heart beating faster?

Its contents were plain and simple. A short narration of her spiritual state, her enjoyment of her new freedom and a verse from her daily reading of the Scripture. She thanked me from the bottom of her heart for rescuing her.

The message swam before my eyes for a moment and all our adventures since the moment old Wynflæd had passed me that first wax tablet seemed to rush past my eyes. Whatever would

Wynflæd say about the turn events had taken? She could have talked on for a year about all that had happened! Then that strange feeling engulfed me again – the inexplicable feeling that I had had before, when I first realised I meant to go through with an escape plan although I had had no idea how to form one. But this time I felt no fear of what I saw in my heart; I was just elated and I knew what I was going to do. Suddenly everything – not just the message on Leofrun's tablet but my whole life – seemed to come into sharp focus. I *had* rescued her; I was not going to spend the rest of my days without her.

"I have a journey to make," I said, steadying myself with an effort and then stowing the tablets briskly inside my jerkin.

Adam and Morcant looked at one another.

"There will always be a home for you and plenty of work, for a plain, efficient carpenter, at Leofham Burgh," said Morcant and Swefred nodded in vigorous agreement, "The place is not half finished yet really," he said.

The little wooden church at Leofham Burgh with its unadorned stone watchtower came, welcome, into my mind. No rood. No flying angels. I knew now that I too needed only the plain words of Scripture. Working at Corvey Abbey in Francia had been a valuable experience I would never forget but now I would rather use my skills to earn my living alongside Guthra. "Thank you," I said, "I hope I will not be long in coming. But I have to go to someone else first."

Morcant raised a quizzical eyebrow.

"I've just solved a riddle," I said.

"What riddle?" asked Adam.

"Why I stole a nun from an Abbey," I said.

# Glossary

| | |
|---|---|
| Aestel | a pointer used to help the reader keep his place when reading from a manuscript |
| Adze | a tool like an axe used for shaping large timbers |
| Allegorical | with a hidden meaning |
| Almoner | a monk whose job was distributing aid to the poor or needy |
| Anagogical | mystical or spiritual |
| Bannocks | flat breads |
| Beeskeps | beehives made of straw or similar materials |
| Benedictine | following the rules laid down by Benedict (480-547) |
| Clerk | someone set apart to be a minster or official of the church |
| Crucifix | an image of Jesus on the cross |
| Dorter | dormitory, sleeping quarters |
| Ealdorman | a high-ranking royal official |
| Ecclesiastical | relating to the church |

| | |
|---|---|
| Fyrd | miltia, defence forces |
| Fyrdman | member of the fyrd |
| Gloss/glosses | annotation or running commentary, interpretation or translation, written alongside the main text of a book |
| Heresy | unbiblical idea(s) |
| Heretic | someone with heretical beliefs |
| Heretical | unbiblical, wrong ideas |
| Hippocampus | sea horse |
| Lay people | everyone not set apart to be a minster or official of the church |
| Liturgy | a standardised form of religious service, which is repeated from memory or may be written down |
| Mercians | inhabitants of Mercia |
| Metaphor | a comparison made by describing one thing in terms of another |
| None | a church service held at mid-afternoon |
| Novice | a trainee monk or nun |
| Offices | religious services |
| Overlord | a ruler with other rulers under him |
| Packhorse | a horse used to carry goods |
| Pallet | a straw mattress or makeshift bed |

# Glossary

*Pater Noster, qui es in caelis, sanctificetur nomen tuum.*
  first line of the Lord's prayer in Latin.

| | |
|---|---|
| Patristic | relating to the early church fathers |
| Penance | a punishment or payment for sins |
| Pottage | a thick soup or stew made from meat or vegetables as available |
| Reeve | a local official or magistrate |
| Scriptorium | a room where books are copied out by hand |
| Sext | a church service held at noon |
| Talisman | a lucky object with magic powers |
| Terce | a church service held at 9 a.m. |
| Thrall | a slave |
| Throstle | thrush |
| Trencher | a flat round of bread, often stale, used as a plate |
| Tropological | figurative, symbolic |
| Vespers | a church service held at sunset |
| Vigils | a church service held the evening before an important day |
| Vowess | a woman who has vowed to remain unmarried, such as a nun |
| Westwerk | a grand entrance, often facing westwards, in medieval Frankish church buildings |

| Wyvern | a winged dragon-like creature with a long tail and often only two legs |

## Places Mentioned in the Story

| Aachen | favourite residence of Charlemagne, King of the Franks (748-814). In modern Germany, close to the borders of Belgium and the Netherlands. Famous for hot springs. |
| Æt Baðum | Bath, a town in Wessex on the border with Mercia. Bath is still famous for its hot spring and the ruins of a Roman bath complex. |
| Corbie | a town in modern France. An Abbey was founded here in c.660 that was famous for its scriptorium q.v. |
| Corvey | a town in modern Germany. An Abbey was founded here by monks from Corbie in 816. The Westwerk is still standing. |
| Danelaw | territory ruled by the Vikings to the north and East of Wessex and its dominions. |
| Francia | the kingdom of the Franks, covering most of modern day France and Germany Partitioned in 843 into West and East Francia. |
| Mercia | Anglo-Saxon kingdom south of the River Humber and centred on the Trent Valley. In Alfred's time it was ruled by an Ealdorman (q.v.) under Alfred. |
| Shaftesbury | Alfred founded a Benedictine nunnery in this Dorset town around 888 and appointed his young daughter abbess. |
| South Sea | the English Channel |

| | |
|---|---|
| Wessex | Anglo-Saxon kingdom in the south of modern England. |

# Wulfgar and the Riddle